Jefferson Manor

One night, One Manor, Three Friends

Elexa Wood

Book Cover by Elexa Wood

1st edition 2024
Book and Cover design by Elexa Wood
ISBN: 979-8-9918476-2-9

First Edition: November 2024

CONTENTS

Chapter One

Henley

Henley Jamison is fully aware that her hometown of Rocky River, Wyoming is a strange eerie place. Between the Halloween rules and the ominous stories kids tell around the bonfires, the town had a knack for making headlines. However, Henley knows this town is what creates her passion for Halloween, and it is also what changes it.

The annual Halloween lockdown, an event that has been occurring Henleys' entire childhood. A lockdown that was created long before she was born just in order to prevent crime. Rocky River Police Department implements a curfew of 9:00 p.m. sharp. However, a select few participants will get to partake in the sleepover at Jefferson Manor. The Jeffersons have a history going back decades of only opening the manor up to others for the course of this one night. The idea behind this concept is to keep people safe on Halloween. However, no one could imagine how popular this sleepover would become. Rocky River and Jefferson Manor merely help create the Halloween tradition for the children in the town. As long as Henley was old enough to understand the event, she begins to anticipates it every year. For a fee of $75 dollars, only fifteen young individuals that are in their Senior year are selected to spend Halloween night in the manor with an enormous feast and an extensive list of Halloween games. This year, however, Henleys' peace along with the town was coming to an end.

Henley knows that her Senior year is going to be the year she shines. Her parents promising her that she can put her name in the drawing to experience the Halloween Haunt sleepover. Henley desperately wishes to be selected as it has been her dream as long as she can remember.

A night where she can doll herself up and enjoy a sleepover with her two best friends Ava and Levi. She remembers meeting Ava and Levi in Elementary school as her family is friends with their family, and they have been the trio ever since. As she looks in the mirror putting on her red lipstick before school. Bright red lipstick is her staple look as it goes well with her fair complexion. Henley is stuck in thought as her doorbell rings, she hurries down to see Levi and Ava waiting impatiently for her.

Levi looks up at her as she opens the front door, running his fingers through his dark brown hair as he sighs jokingly and says "Ms. Henley are you ready to grace the world with your appearance?"

Ava softly pushes Levi out of the way. "Ah, come on Le give her a break."

Ava winking at Henley handing her donut holes from

Ollie O's bakery. Henley grabs her backpack, yelling bye to her mom as she rushes out the door. Levi finally getting a vehicle has really saved them so much time when going to school. It is only fitting that his first car is a jet black lifted 2020 Ford Raptor. A truck that screams the bad boy persona he is trying to portray.

"So, Henley, are we getting our tickets for Halloween Haunt today?" Levi questions as he hops in the driver seat.

"Sure, we may want to get them today so we can be the first names in the drawing." Henley agrees.

Ava chimes in from the backseat. "I hear this year is supposed to be the best yet."

Little did the three childhood friends know that this year will ultimately decide the course of the rest of their lives.

While Levi and Ava go on about their activities of the morning ranging from Levi's daily 5:00 a.m. workout to Ava's new coffee flavor, Henley couldn't help but become intrigued by the scenery on the way to school.

The colors of Halloween are here, the yellows and the oranges of the falling trees are her favorite. Even though their town was small, it is beautiful this time of the year. Mayor Sampson thrives on Halloween, so every year he makes sure the decorations of scarecrows, pumpkins, and ghosts are up to his visions. Henley loves that she gets to enjoy such a Halloween thrill. From the 20-foot pumpkin man in the middle of the courthouse, to the miniature skeleton yard stakes there is never a spot that is untouched.

Henley notices a man she never has seen before standing by the courtyard gazebo dressed in all black. His piercing eyes staring at her as they wait at a red light. I know everyone in this town, Henley thinks. Her mind is full of astonishment as no one ever moves to this town due to the size and there is little growth. Secretly, Henley loves this.

Ava nudges her saying, "Earth to Henley, have you heard me at all?"

"No, sorry, what were you saying?" Henley inquires, turning around to look at Ava.

"I was saying," Ava continues without missing a beat, "Jake is asking a lot about you in History class."

Henley sees Le glance up through the rearview mirror at Ava as Henley says, "ehh he isn't really my type."

Le and Ava have been giving strange looks to one another, usually when Ava mentions a boy Henley silently thinks.

Le snaps, "Well Jake isn't a good guy at all for Henley anyways." Ava just shrugs as she sits back in the seat.

They make it to the parking lot with just 10 minutes before first period. Time doesn't seem to exist during October, as the teachers usually give leeway since there is such an increase in traffic due to people visiting for all Mayor Sampsons decorations. Le rushes out of the truck yelling, "Let's meet by the middle lockers after 1st to get our tickets."

"Sure!" Henley exclaims as she grabs Ava to make it to class before the bell.

Henley slams into her seat next to Gwen, Toby, and Nikki just as the bell chimes. Henly lets out an exhausting sign as she sits, she is always pushing her luck with almost being late.

Gwen and Nikki have been thick as thieves as long as Henley can remember. Toby always silently following Gwen around like a lost puppy, something he has done since grade school. Henley clashes with Gwen and her crew for as long as she can remember, but luckily, they only have one period together. Ms. Lynn, their AP Calculus teacher comes rushing in almost as if she is afraid of being later herself. Ms. Lynn, a small lady with blonde curls in her mid-50s is always so cheerful. A spirit Henley hopes to have when she is her age. Henley tries to focus on AP Calculus, but can't seem to wrap her mind around all the numbers and calculations due to her anxiety. Impatiently, she taps her legs as she waits for the bell to ring.

Finally, the bell sounds, Henley excitedly rushes out the hall passing the homecoming banners. The idea to run for homecoming and coerce people into voting for her never appealed to Henley. She turns the corner and hits Levi in the chest.

"Girl, I know you missed me but damn slow down." Levi jokes as he winks.

"Oh, shut up, you are the one who told me to meet you," Henley says.

She turns away from him and begins walking to the line for the tickets so Levi doesn't see her blushing. Lately, Levi has been looking very handsome with his bad boy image she thinks as they file into line with everyone else. They overhear Ava rushing through the line squeezing to get to them. This has become her new normal as she is always late.

"Woo, glad y'all were already in line." Ava exclaims.

They wait impatiently as they make their way through the lines. Finally, they reach the front and hurriedly pay their fees while scribbling down their names. The receptionist says the date of the drawing is in the town square and that will take place two days from now at 1:00 p.m. Henley quickly does her good luck rub on the piece of paper as she places it in the goblet containing at least 100 pieces of papers already. Le and Ava are both very negative towards the idea that they will get picked but Henleys gut feeling is telling her that she will get to fulfill her dream.

Henley separates ways with her friends and makes her way to her history class. As Professor James goes on and on about the Cold War, Henley immerses herself in her thoughts of only having two days until the drawing. After the drawing if she and her friends are selected, she will be playing scary games and watching Halloween movies in the Jefferson Manor in no time. There is only one problem so far, and that is she has no idea what to wear. She could wear something that she already has, but what is the fun in that? She decides she must get something new, something flashy. She always takes Ava to go shopping with her. Henley loves getting her styling tips from Ava who is on top of the latest trends. Although Halloween is Henleys passion, she knows deep down that this sleepover is not only to celebrate the night in a creepy manor but also to serve as one last Halloween to spend with Le and Ava before college.

Finally, History is over. As she gathers her books, she looks up to see Jake coming to her.

"Hey Hen, are you going to the drawing for the Halloween Haunt?"

"Of course!" Henley says, trying to control her shock in her voice.

"Well, great can't wait to see you there," he says as he sits down.

Henley can't help but wonder why he's talking to her

now. He never talks to her; in all the years they have known one another. There must be a reason. Maybe Ava was right, maybe he does have a crush on her. She could envision dating him, but she also knows how she feels about Levi.

Henley makes it through her next period while gossiping about her and Jake's encounter in the hallways. Ava fusses and Levi just shrugs it off. She admits that Levi does seem a little jealous, but he always gets like that when she mentions guys. Henley continues to ponder on her and Levi's relationship throughout the day. She finally reaches her last period, as she wonders how she is going to make it through the rest of the week before the event. Her last class is Cell Biology, a subject she has no interest in. She lets her mind wonder to if Levi will ever get enough courage to ask her out. Would she say yes, or would her concerns with ruining their friendship overwhelm her? Henley is so stuck in her thoughts of Levi she almost misses the bell to leave.

She hurriedly rushes out to Levi's truck to see him patiently leaning against the door with his hands shoved in his pockets. He raises his head up just as she is about to reach him as his brown curl falls over his forehead and his devilish handsome smile comes out, as he swoops her up in his arms swinging her around in the air. This has become one of Henleys' favorite things that Levi does. It creates an intimate bond between them. Henley can feel his pulsating heartbeat as her fingers linger down his chest as he places her back on the ground. Their eyes meet for a split second as she can feel a slight blush rise to her cheeks. He turns around to open the truck door for her.

On the way home, Henley asks Ava to go with her on Friday after school so she can pick out the perfect outfit for

Saturday night. Ava reluctantly agrees because shopping was not something Ava wants to do on a Friday. But she knows Henley needs her help, especially since Ava can feel this Halloween sleepover could be the start of something serious for her best friends. Levi always drops Ava off at home first, because he lives closer to Henley. However, Ava knows secretly it is because he wants more alone time with her.

Ava scurries out of the truck, as she screams "See ya, goons!" as she reaches her door.

Levi puts the truck in reverse, as he smiles and asks Henley, "So, how was your day?"

Henley secretly loves their little time they have together before dropping her off. She goes through her daily activities, and tells him of her big outfit idea. Levi is always such a good listener, even if it was a topic he didn't care for. They pull up to her house just in time to see her dad pulling up. She hugs Levi and grabs her backpack as she gets out beaming with excitement to tell her family she put her name in the goblet. She turns to wave bye at Levi, as he always waits for the wave before leaving.

Her parents share their enthusiasm about her entry to the sleepover as they discuss over dinner what the rules are. These rules include the basics: no drinking, no drugs, and keep your cell phone charged. She doesn't understand why they always say no drugs or no drinking, given that this is not something that particularly interests Henley anyways, unlike most the kids at school. But she only ever hangs out with Levi and Ava, and they don't do this either. She knows that her parents are just being cautious.

The next few days at school fly by in a blur, Henley knowing full well she did not register anything from her classes during that time. She cannot even recall the conversations she had with Levi and Ava. Usually something she can remember verbatim. It is almost like those days leading up to the drawing day her body and her mind were just going through the motions. A time that feels almost lost to her.

She excitedly reaches the drawing day, the day she has been waiting for most of her life. The school lets out at 12:30 p.m., just enough time for her, Levi, and Ava to rush to the Town Square. As the school parking lot overcrowds with their classmates, Levi hops in the driver side as he motions with his hand for Ava and Henley to hurry up. The girls get in, Henley bouncing with excitement unable to control her anticipation.

Ava jumps in her seat as she exclaims, "You guys, this is it. This is what we have waited on!"

"Surely the stars will align and we'll all get picked," Le declares. They slowly make their way behind the traffic jam to get to the Town Square. Henley bounces her legs in the passenger seat as they edge closer and closer to the parking lot.

Le says, "Come on girl, I've never seen you this excited."

Henley just rolls her eyes and smirks. The slowness of the traffic mixed with their eagerness creates the feeling they are not moving at all.

Finally, they reach the parking lot as Le tries to maneuver through the crowds of people.

"Well, we're here. Are you guys ready?" Le asks as he pulls into the parking spot.

Henley and Ava both squeal. "Yes!" while hopping out

and running up the cobblestone sidewalk not even looking back or waiting on Levi.

As they push themselves through the crowd, more people entered than Henley could even imagine. Given their slim figures, Henley and Ava are able to squeeze through most of the people making it to the stage just in time. Mayor Sampson standing at the podium smiling ear to ear as he pulls the first slip of paper out and begins stating her classmates' names. Henley tunes out the crowd until she begins to hear Ava's name called. Ava and Henley both hug each other enthusiastically as Levi finally finds them. Le congrats Ava with a high-five as they interestedly wait for the other names. Henley clutches Le's hand out of instinct as Mayor Sampson pulls another card out of the goblet.

The names begin to come and go as it rounds up to the last few names. She glances over at Ava frowning as she sadly thinks that her best friend might be the only one who goes. She hears Levis' name as she looks at his stunned face as Ava hits his arm in excitement. Le grips Henleys' hand harder as he slowly realizes she may not be able to go. Henley feels herself getting overwhelmed as more names are selected. They're now down to the last name, the last drawing. Mayor Sampson finally announces Henleys' name as Ava and Le tackle her. Could this be real? They all get to go. Henley thinks to herself that it is a weird coincidence.

After the awe and shock wears off, the 15 selected now must go up to the stage to get their tickets. Henley, Levi and Ava all run up to the stage where they see the tickets laid out on the table. Henley is finally holding her dark green ticket with orange shimmering writing glistening as the manor illuminates in the background of the ticket. She steps aside waiting for Levi and Ava to get their tickets. Of course, as soon as they get their tickets the three of them snap a quick selfie.

On Friday, the day of shopping Henley anxiously waits for Levi to pick her up. She begins to wonder how lucky they are that they will fulfill their childhood dream. This must be some kind of miracle that the stars aligned; Henley thinks as she hears Le pull up. Le reluctantly drives the girls to Main Street to partake in a shopping adventure. He is always doing small things like this for them. They reach the boutique, as Henley and Ava excitedly rush in, almost knocking over the ladies exiting. Levi apologizes with a smirk and a shrug. The girls make a beeline to the nearest rack of clothes as Levi slumps down in the nearest swivel recliner pulling out his phone. Henley goes through the rack of clothes frequently looking for something that catches her eyes. She grabs a small leather jacket, a green top, a holey pair of jeans and black booties. She enters the dressing room just as Ava tosses a maroon shirt over the top with a low collar.

"Try this on with the same outfit, then come show us." She orders.

Henley looks in the mirror as her blonde curls fall over the leather jacket, and she smirks as she opens the door.

Ava immediately jumps up and down. "Yes, that is it!"

Ava quickly turns Levis' recliner around as he starts to protest, she says "Shh, don't you dare peek!" Ava rushes to Henley grabbing her arm guiding her to the mirror. Henley must admit she does look slighter older and the colors of this outfit go so well together. This is the one, the outfit that in that moment she feels will make her transition from a girl to a woman.

She makes it up to the cashier as the lady says "$87.72 please?"

As Henley reaches for her card, Levi softly places his card on the table and says "Early birthday present."

He winks at Henley. Henley begins to object but knows it will do no good, Levi wouldn't change his mind. She thanks him.

As he shrugs nonchalantly and says "My pleasure." He grabs her bags to carry them out.

As they make it back to the truck, Levi suggests sushi for dinner, and they both agree. Sushi was their little thing; they have always gone to the same place together since they were 10. They make it to the restaurant, to see Jake's mustang in the parking lot.

Ava says, "Oh yes Jake is here, as Levi groans hopping out to open both Ava and I doors.

"Ya know y'all would probably be great buds if y'all just talk." Ava says as she grabs Henley's arm to go in.

Henley jokes, "Sounds like you've got a little crush on Jake."

Ava blushes and throws her hands in the air trying to shrug off the suggestion.

The restaurant was busier today, more than usual as the three make it to their booth. Levi slides in as Henley sits beside him.

Ava goes to Jake's table to say a quick hello, as Levi snickers "Ya know she is going to be hanging out with him all night." The waiter comes to the table as they order three waters, and the fried calamari appetizer.

"So, Levi, who are you excited to hang with all night?"

Henley digs hoping to get an answer from him.

"Well Hen, of course you!" he jokes as he does his sly smirk.

Henley rolls her eyes. "Oh, come on you always say that."

"Maybe one day you will know it's the truth." He quickly snaps back as he looks deeply into Henley green eyes. A moment she will never forget, just as Ava slams down in the booth.

Ava blurting out, "Well Jake is bringing Red Bulls for the haunt."

"Of course, he is," Levi jokes, "the tool drink." As they banter back and forth, Henley glances around to see the same man she saw two mornings ago, sitting by himself in the booth in the corner.

"Do you guys know that man?" Henley breaks up the bickering.

Levi looks over. "Oh yeah, that's Old Man Jones. "Yeah, you know that's the man with bodies in his closet," he whispers as he tickles Henley.

"Oh stop, is that Old Man Jones?" Henley asks, thinking he looks different than when she saw him as a kid.

"Yes ma'am." Ava says as she grabs the straw for her water.

Levi reassuringly says "yes just an old man that is the bud of all little kids' stories."

Levi and Ava go back to talking about random things as Henleys' mind wanders to when they were kids. Old Man Jones always held the title as the creepy old man in the town. As children, Henley could picture those nights like they were yesterday. All sitting around the bonfire, listening to the outlandish stories of what Old Man Jones did to his family. Stories ranging from cutting his wife up and serving her as pumpkin pie on Halloween, to how he left his family in the woods off Elk Road 33 to fend for themselves. No one really knows the story; they're just trained to stay away from him. But as Henley is looking at him now, she doesn't feel anxious or scared, she feels a sting of pity for him as he eats alone.

She is shaken back to reality as her food arrives. Levi, Ava, and Henley make it through their entrees as Levi orders his normal which consists of every dessert on the menu. A tradition Levi has done for years, always stating "Women should always have options."

"Hey, why don't we give Old Man Jones some dessert?" Henley suggests. She shrugs off Ava's and Levi's look of bewilderment as she says, "What, dessert cheers up people." Levi and Ava look at Old Man Jones.

"Well, sure why not?" Levi chuckles, "but I'm not taking it over there."

"I will," Henley says as she gets up, not waiting for Levi to protest. She picks up the chocolate mousse cake and makes her way to his table. She can feel Levi's eyes watching her every move ready to jump to her defense if need be.

Unsure of his real name, Henley feels her voice shaking as she says, "Sir, our table thought you may enjoy some dessert on us. Everyone likes chocolate."

Old Man Jones grudgingly looks up, as his eyes meet Henley's. She feels a chill go through her spine as his gray eyes look straight through her. "Well lady, I do appreciate the gesture. Just know, you helped me make my decision."

Henley about to ask what he means just as a clash from

behind interrupts her. A waiter quickly apologizing to the crowd. Henley briskly helping the waiter pick up the broken plates, as she turns back around, she sees Old Man Jones pushing his chair in as he tips his hat to Henley and walks out.

Henley slumps down next to Levi as he snickers, "Well, is it too soon to say you sure know how to clear a room out?" He rubs her leg while smirking at her.

Ava goes back to her pumpkin pie, as she decides to change the subject. "So, you guys our big night is only two days away, and I'm going to kiss Jake that night.

Levi almost spits out his water and incredulously says, "Girl, have y'all even talked or are you just going in for the punch?"

"We've talked." Ava snaps, "Plus, he is a jock so I got to swoop in before some cheerleader gets him." Ava brushes her brown curls back over her ear, as her piercing blue eyes look at Henley. A look Henley knows well, the look of determination.

"Well Ava, you go get your man," Henley excitedly says.

Levi leaves to pay the tab as Ava asks "Henley are you going to tell Le you like him, or do I have too?"

"I don't like him, plus we have known each other way too long," Henley snaps quickly trying to hide her blushing.

"That's why y'all are perfect!" Ava exclaims, as Henley stands up grabbing her coat.

"Let's go, no more talk of this." Henley says as Levi comes back

"Are my two favorite girls ready?" Levi asks.

The ride home that night was eerily quiet. Ava in her

thoughts about Jake and her first real kiss. Or the hopes of her first real kiss on Halloween. Levi stealing side looks at Henley, wanting to say so much but not able to form any words. Her hair glowing in the moonlight as he drives past the streetlights.

Henley's mind racing back and forth to that night and her feelings around the diner. It seems so different, the night in itself seems so off. But Henley couldn't put her finger on what she was feeling. So lost in her mind, she almost forgot to tell Ava bye as she got out of the truck. Levi and Henley surprisingly set in silence the short ride to her home. She didn't even do her signature wave as she hurried out.

Henley can't get out of her head what Old Man Jones said to her all night.

Why would he say something like that? So cryptic and weird, and those eyes were so gloomy. Lost in her thoughts she forgot to show her mom her outfit they picked out, she decides she will first thing before school.

She snatches her laptop off her desk, as she types in Old Man Jones in the search engine. Numerous new stories start popping up, ones about his divorce, and ones about his kids' bodies being found on Halloween night. "Two boys, one girl found in the mine off of 33, mother is nowhere to be found," the headline says. Henley feels that same chill course through her veins she felt earlier that night.

Two of the three children would have been in their grade, and now that Henley thinks about it, she doesn't recall ever meeting the mother. Although, she does remember the kids vaguely. One boy, Collin the oldest, was just a grade above Henley, and the twins Cash and Cate. She remembers playing with them at the parks. Old Man Jones was always around but never the mother, even when people would try to invite her to neighborhood events or community events, she would never come. But, why? She never sat down and thought about it before. She wonders if her parents had ever met the mother or went to school with her. They would have been around the same age.

The bodies being found became a town horror story that no one talks about. Henley was so young when it happened, she hardly remembers. Henley's train of thought is interrupted by her phone dinging the normal "Goodnight Best Friend" text from Levi. Something he has done since they got their cellphones.

"Goodnight bestie," Henley types as she puts her phone down for the night.

As she turns back to her laptop, she sees an article that catches her by surprise. "Psychologist Derek Jones shuts down practice after the wake of his children's bodies being found." A picture of Derek Jones is shown on the cover. The same piercing gray eyes, except on a younger man, Henley thinks as she clicks the article. Wow, this is Old Man Jones? She wonders. Stunned by the fact that this man was a psychologist, a man of integrity it seems. As she reads through the article, she learns that Derek Jones was a tough but wealthy psychologist on the brink of greatness before his family's horror story tragically halted his career.

The article ends with showing a picture of the family of five standing outside his practice smiling ear to ear. Mrs. Jones, a beautiful young woman with long black curls, sitting proudly next to her three children all with blonde curls and baby blue eyes. A picturesque family as it appears. Henley shudders at the idea that such a tragic event occurred to this family, but no one really ever got an explanation. Old Man Jones seemed to lock himself in his house after, and only makes appearances during the month of October. Which in itself is creepy enough, Henley thinks as she yawns and shuts her laptop.

Henley tossing and turning all night with visions of her and Old Man Jones kids. Visions of them playing with her in the park, visions of the kids coming to sleepovers at her house, and visions of them playing hopscotch on the sidewalk. She is awoken by her alarm clock going off at 7:00 a.m. Exhausted, she raises up. Her dreams had to come from somewhere, but she is completely unsure of how and why she was having these visions. She doesn't remember being extremely close to the Jones Children. Or even really every hanging out with them. She shrugs it off and gets up out of bed to go downstairs to eat breakfast with her family, a little tradition of theirs.

Turning the oven on medium heat as she grabs the eggs and pancakes mix from the refrigerator, she turns around to see her dad and little brother coming in from the back yard.

"Hey, Dad. Hey, Sebastian, breakfast will be ready in 30," she happily says as Sebastian sits at the bar. Her dad chats to her about his early morning as Sebastian plays on his phone. Sebastian and Henley have always been close with only being one year apart. They were inseparable growing up. They even resemble each other in looks with the same blonde hair and dark green eyes; however, they act completely opposite.

Mornings are always special since most of the time they are all running in opposite directions, Sebastian with his weightlifting, Henley with school and friends, her dad being a head prosecutor for the county and her mom being the judge, it is never easy to be all together at once. Breakfast time has become the time where everyone discusses their weeks, from dad's upcoming workload, mom's upcoming trials, and Sebastian upcoming college scouts.

Henley chimes in this morning, curious about Old Man Jones story, as she asks, "Hey, do y'all remember the Derek Jones case?"

Her dad shoots her a sharp look, a look that Henley knows well. A look of this is a weird question mixed with why are we discussing a topic that you shouldn't know about. Her mom stops dead in her tracks from bringing the plates of pancakes over. Sebastian is clueless to their behavior.

Sebastian has always been oblivious to his surroundings, as he pours himself another glass of coffee. Henley suddenly backtracking based on the awkward responses and contemplates a reason for her asking very quickly.

"I saw him at the diner last night and he was all by himself. He looked kind of sad, do you know if he has any family?" she asks, hoping this will soothe the sharp look from her dad.

Her dad sighing, "Honey, he just doesn't have anyone, but he is used to it."

Her mom jumps in saying, "Yeah Henley, it isn't nice to pry into someone's life. Some people are just better off alone."

And with that breakfast commences to normal conversations.

While grabbing her bag to leave, Henley decides she is going to find out who Old Man Jones is by herself, but right now she doesn't have time to worry about it. She has to get ready for the big Halloween event. Due to the event, and Halloween falling on a Saturday this year, the school is letting out early again today. Henley rushes saying bye to her family as she hears Levi's truck come up. He has started a new trend of coming to the door recently. Henley is not sure why, but she wants to avoid this. So, she darts out the door before he has a chance to pull up.

Levi puts the car in park as he steps out, looking more handsome than ever to her and smiles his dashing smile. Henley wonders when he became so good looking.

"Good morning, Hen," he says as he meets her at the passenger door to open.

"Hey loser," she jokes as she hops in.

"Where is Ava?" Henley asks as Levi gets in.

"Oh, I have a surprise for you, so I already dropped her off at school," Levi says as his blue eyes pierce into her soul.

"Le, it's not my birthday." She jokes.

"You're right, " he says, "but it is your favorite holiday so you should at least get something."

Levi drives to the gazebo in the middle of the town, and Henley can't believe what she sees. It is decorated with the most beautiful flowers alongside the normal Fall decorations. Henley sees in the middle of the gazebo a white blanket with donuts and her favorite drink from Starbucks.

"What is this?" Henley asks as Levi opens her door and reaches for her hand to let her out.

"Well, ya see this is a big year for all of us, we all get to go to Halloween night and I just figured what better way to start off our weekend then with your favorite things," he says.

"That is sweet, Le," Henley says as she starts blushing looking away.

Henley can't believe what she's seeing. She has only ever seen this kind of thought and emotion in a movie. The romantic movies she remembers her and Levi making fun of when they were younger. She had no idea Levi is so romantic but then again why would she. How did she get so lucky to have him on her side? She knows deep down she is falling for him quicker and quicker. Henley doesn't even want to stop it anymore. They spend the next hour discussing their plans for the sleepover to their plans for prom, and he even listens to her crazy theories about Old Man Jones.

Levi was always good at listening and making plans with her. It had been a while since she and Levi had a chance to hang out with just one another. It is crazy how much she didn't know about him or how much has changed about him. She studies his face shape and how it has matured over just the last year. The top of his hair falls more down on his forehead now. She always jokes that his hair resembles Elvis or James Dean. His eyes have turned much more into a crystal blue instead of the dark blue they used to be. As much as she has tried not to like him more than just the friend he was, she couldn't help it. Even though Henley can see how Levi treats her differently than every other girl, she can't seem to accept the fact he likes her. She always feels like it is impossible even though his action shows otherwise. She isn't good with rejection so even when everyone says he is into her she swears it off, just because she doesn't want to get hurt.

After packing up their stuff, Levi asked if he could pick her up for the Halloween party.

"Of course," she exclaimed, "I figured you already were."

In that moment, she sees a glimpse of sadness in his eyes before he flashes his grin and says "Great!"

Henley is not sure why he suddenly got sad by her response. The car ride to school was eerily silent as she could feel Levi recalculating her response. They made it to school right before the bell rang, he left in a rush saying he would meet her after 4th period.

Henley's mind couldn't focus throughout the day, she couldn't get Old Man Jones out of her head. What was so bad that her parents needed to hide the truth? I mean she knows his family died and the mother disappeared. She is aware that Old Man Jones isolates himself because of this. But there had to be a reason and surely a bigger explanation. She begins to wonder about all the eerie stories she heard growing up. As she is thinking of everything, she comes to the realization that this town in itself is extremely weird. Not only did they have Old Man Jones, but this town was filled with similar stories of Rambling Ronnie, Freakshow Freddie, and Sad Eyes Sally. All these names were given by kids just so they could tell scary stories.

Henley, completely trapped in her thoughts wonders why she never investigated further into the town's stories. As she recalls these stories, she realizes there were so many inconsistencies that never occurred to her. But where had these people gone? She is used to seeing Old Man Jones every October, that being the only month he came out of his house on Maple drive. But the others she hasn't seen or heard about in a while or maybe she just hasn't been looking. Her mind flashes back to all the stories she heard growing up. Rambling Ronnie telling stories of his childhood on the streets to bystanders. The rumors of his rich wealthy parents physically and mentally abusing him throughout his life. He has a few loose screws so no one ever truly believed him. In reality, his family is one of the most admired members of the community. Sadly, them being so high up in the community made it extremely hard to believe Rambling Ronnie's allegations. Ronnie has a history of drugs at an early age which not only made him an outcast to his family but it created an even dimmer light on his character. He was so sporadic in nature that the town just assumed he was just a bad seed.

Freakshow Freddie a victim of a terrible childhood which resulted in him getting caught up in the carnival. He attempted to escape his life but his mind became a dungeon of torment. He was so consumed in how bad his life was that he ultimately lost track of his personality by creating multiple different personas in his head. He eventually got placed in the mental institution on Garrison Drive. Henley realizes when he was placed in the mental institution that was the last that she heard about him.

Henley almost forgot the story that made her the saddest. Sad-eyed Sally, a poor widow of a wealthy doctor that use to wander around having conversations with her deceased husband. A woman who continued to search for her dead soulmate through the streets late at night.

How truthful were the stories? Henley thinking to

herself.

The bell rings for second period and she rushes to grab her things, she feels her body fill with excitement that the day is almost over.

Henley blurs through the next two classes as she goes back and forth from nervousness for the Halloween party to excitement to see Levi and Ava and spend her favorite holiday with them. At the thought of Levi and her staying the night together she begins to get anxious. Yes, she had stayed with him before when they were in diapers. However, with his newfound looks and charm, Henley couldn't help but feel anxious.

After school, she rushes out of the classroom to see Levi waiting for her at the door. His grin spreading ear to ear as he says "Ms. Henley are you ready to enjoy your dream?" and reaches for her hand. They hurriedly rush down the hall to Ava's class.

They find her impatiently waiting outside the door of her Algebra class. "For being so ecstatic it took y'all long enough," laughing as she swings her backpack up from the ground.

"Well, I can't control the bells," Henley jokingly states. The three try to navigate through the crowd as quickly as possible to the parking lot. Finally, as they push through the black stained double doors to exit the school, Henley can't help but notice the cheerleaders eyeing Levi with an immense look of lust in their eyes. She wonders how he doesn't seem to notice them.

Ava asking, "So are we going to "Delicious Dough" tonight?"

"Well of course, Levi says, "that's how we'll end the

night. I will pick both of y'all up at 3:00 p.m. tomorrow. It will take us about 45 minutes to get to the Halloween manor." Levi is a planner, a trait that Henley loves about him. He always had the plan laid out before she even has to worry or ask about it. It makes Henleys' life so much easier.

They make it to the ice cream parlor just before it gets too busy. This parlor in particular was designed to create an old-fashioned vintage vibe. The walls were decorated with Elvis, Marilyn Monroe, and James Dean decorations. Immersed with bright red vinyl booths and black glass tables. It was the spot to be for high schoolers especially on the night before Halloween. The parlor has a history of always going over the top with gory and bloody decorations. Each table is delicately touched with a pumpkin centerpiece that guests could enjoy carving.

Ever since the trio was young, they always carve the pumpkin and decide who could take it home. Only teenagers came here, which is why it was so strange to see Old Man Jones sitting in the back with a few people she does not recognize. No one seems to notice, but Henley. She brushes this off. It is just because she was thinking about him.

They all glance up as Levi, Henley and Ava enter, but none of them make eye contact except for Old Man Jones. Henley feels his piercing grey eyes look into her soul as she slides into the booth next to Levi. For a split second she catches a glimpse of his children in his facial features. She gathers her thoughts as the waitress asks for her order, Henley ordering her favorite waffle cone covered in the mix of chocolate and vanilla ice cream drizzled with Oreo syrup. Henley decides she is going to enjoy her night, instead of worrying about Old Man Jones and who on earth the other three individuals are in the booth across the way from them. They are just harmless. So, she thought.

The trio enjoys their ice cream while watching the massive tv across from their booth. The diner deciding this year to play the Halloween movie franchise. A movie Henley loves as her eyes beam with excitement as the theme song begins to play. Levi knowing that this simply would top Henley's night catches her eyes glistening with so much joy he can't help but smile.

Ava signs heavily. "Guys, let's not make it obvious."

Henley bashfully looking at Levi as he twiddles his thumbs underneath the table. A characteristic he picked up shortly after his mom left. Her mind wanders back to that time in his life, they were so young yet they had to mature so fast because of it.

Before her mind could stop her mouth, she asks "Do you ever think about your mom Le?" She sees Ava uncomfortably sit up in the booth as she says "Henley." Almost in hopes of stopping her.

Le looks up at Ava as he turns to Henley and says "Well, honestly all the time." He sighs as he continues "I think about why she left. Why she couldn't take me with her. If she had stayed would my life have been any different. Would my dad not be a drunk. He put his hands on the table as his shoulders slump and he says "so to answer your question, yes I do."

Ava trying to soften the air, "Well she missed out on one of the greatest people I know."

As she gently touches his hand. Henley sees tears in the corners of his eyes as she instantly regrets asking. She chimes up "how about we go to the lake tonight, we haven't done that in forever?"

She knows Levi loves the lake especially at night time where they can look at the stars and the moon.

Ava excitedly agrees, as Levi slightly smiles and says "Whatever you girls want." Henley is glad the topic is over. "Well, it's a date, let's go."

They say goodbye to the owners and thank them for everything before making their way to the entrance. The parking lot is illuminated by the streetlights and the moonlight. Ava twirling on her way to the truck like a kid who has had too much sugar, Henley swaying in the breeze as she walks behind Ava giggling from time to time. And Levi steadily behind watching his two best friends taking in the glee of the moment.

The ride to the lake is quiet, almost peaceful. The trio just in a trance of remembrance as they cross the bridge that leads to the lake. A bridge that they use to walk hand and hand across because of fear they would slip through the creaky wood, Henley thinks to herself smiling. Levi pulls up to a spot just underneath the big oak tree that is consuming the path leading to the pond.

Henley hops out as Ava is already running to the bridge. Levi meeting Henley at the front of the truck as he holds his hand out to her. Henley clasping it energetically as they walk down to the bridge. They make their spot on the side dangling their feet in the water. The three past the next couple hours pointing at the stars, watching the moon glistening on the water and reminiscing about their childhood.

As the night progresses, they realize it is time to head

home, the car ride goes by fast as the trio continues to laugh and enjoy one another's company. A ride that appears just like every other car ride, but deep-down Henley feels this ride is different.

Dropping Ava off first per the usual, she hugs Henley gleefully saying "love you girl" before stepping out of the truck and running up the stone sidewalk.

On the way to Henleys' house, the two reminisce on the night and how ecstatic they are for sleepover. As they reach Henley's white and black brick home, Henley feels a burst of yearning lust come over her. A feeling she has continued to shove down every time Levi and her are alone. Like the gentleman he always is, he walks around and opens the door. In the moonlight she sees her reflection in his eyes and at that moment she can't hold it back any longer.

"I like you Le," she blurts out so fast she doesn't have time to stop herself. She blushes as she glances up to meet his eyes.

He does his nervous smile, as he says well "Hen, I like you too."

"No no," Henley stuttering trying to cover up her nerves. "I don't mean like a friend, I mean more. But I know we will never be anything more so let's just drop it." Henley instantly regretting she said anything as she looks down to pick at her nails.

He grabs her side and says, "Yes, Hen. I know, I also mean more than a friend." She feels his breath so close as he leans in and pecks her forehead. He leans back and says, "Get inside, it is getting late." He shuts the passenger door and watches her walk up the steps.

Sebastian is sitting at the table when she comes in, he

looks up and smiles as he says "You look gleeful."

Henley blushing as she snaps, "Oh, shut up." She grabs water as she runs up her room. She is unsure how she feels because she knows they can't date. If it doesn't last long, it could ruin their decade of friendship. She is slumming in her thoughts as she packs her bag for Halloween night. She sees her phone light up as Ava's ringtone comes blaring out.

"So, Hen, are you ready for tomorrow?" she chimes oblivious to the fact that Henley night just ended so romantically.

"Oh yea, are you?" Henley asks back. She vaguely hears Ava going on and on about tomorrow as she keeps thinking about Levi.

Ava says, "So when were you going to tell me about Le?"

Henley asking innocently, "What do you mean?"

"Oh girl, I know you two had a moment," Ava states. Of course, she does, Henley thinks. Levi would have told her.

"Well, I am nervous, I can't let it turn into anything more," Henley replies blushing it off.

Ava giving her the logical girl response, "It can be anything you want it to be, just think on it. I'll see you tomorrow. Bye girl!" And with that Ava is gone. Henley puts her phone down as she decides it is time for some sleep.

Chapter Two

Levi

Levi is completely taken back at Henley telling him she likes him. He secretly wishes he would have done this sooner. He couldn't contain his excitement; already calling Ava on his way home to tell her everything.

As he sits in his driveway thinking about his day, his mind wanders back to the gazebo breakfast date. A date that was in the works for months. He remembers that morning just watching Henley and getting caught up in her crazy theories and plans. He secretly loves the fact that Henley can count on him but he wishes she noticed the things he does for her and only her. Yes, it was the normal plan for him to pick up Ava and Henley for the sleepover, but he just wishes she would appreciate it more. Her response was a mere sting because he was in a roundabout way asking her as his date to the sleepover, not just a friend. However, he still gets to go with his two favorite girls and Levi in that moment decides that is all that matters.

He recognizes he is falling in love with Henley, even though he probably won't let himself fall harder. He knows deep down; it wouldn't work but he still wants it too. Her blonde hair always falling so loosely on her shoulders, it is like she doesn't even have to try. Her green eyes constantly memorize him, it is like looking out into an open field. It creates a sense of peace for him. It always has. A sense of peace that he has longed for most of his life.

Consumed in his thoughts, he finally looks up to see his dark home. No lights on at all. His dad wasn't home yet, which honestly isn't a surprise for Levi but he still feels a sting of sadness. His dad works a lot and also loves the bar a lot more. His dad is a great man, however since his mom left his dad completely lost his way. His dad is always trying to overcompensate with buying Levi nice things, or letting Levi do whatever he wants without any questions. Levi always wonders if it is his dads attempt to try to make him forget he doesn't have a mother.

He decides to finally go inside to let his dog outside. A dog he absolutely adores, a dog his dad got him on his eighth birthday to make up for the fact his mom left him on his seventh birthday. A day he doesn't like to think about. Everyone around him knows not to mention his mother, so it is extremely odd that Henley asked about her tonight. He usually gets angry, but with Henley and Ava it is different. They were there. They held him in the road as he slumped to his knees watching her drive away. Leaving behind her family to go chase the California sun. Without Henley and

Ava, Levi honestly feels like he wouldn't have made it. This is a bond that can never be broken between the three.

He illuminates the kitchen with lights as he makes his way to the refrigerator to grab a snack. His mind scanning the room seeing all the times throughout his life he saw his dad standing at the bar countertop in the corner of the house, overlooking their flower bed. A flower bed his mother loved so dearly. A flower bed that his dad has ultimately let die. Levi remembers the nights where he would hear his father on the phone searching for his mother, calling everyone they knew. Eventually his father gave up, but that never stopped Levi from wondering where she was out there. Did she have another family, or did he have any siblings?

Levi's thoughts are interrupted with the sound of the microwave dinging. He pulls his food out as he reaches for his phone to send his famous goodnight text to his two favorite girls.

Chapter Three

Henley

Today was finally the day her and the rest of the town have been waiting for. Henley wakes up about 10:00 a.m. in just enough time to eat lunch with her family and finish getting ready before Levi and Ava to pick her up at 3:00 p.m. While Henley changes clothes, she glances over at her laptop and sees the research she was doing on Old Man Jones a couple of days ago. She almost forgot her pulsating obsession with the old tales they told as a kid. She glances down at her phone as Levi's message comes through. "Good morning, Hen! Today is the day! Can't wait to see you at 3!" Henley ponders on the idea of how weird it is that he hasn't said anything about their kiss, but pushes it aside as she types "Good morning! See you then!" she puts her phone down as she opens Google on her laptop.

She types in Ronnie Posey, and her screen is immediately filled with headlines of his life. "Young boy Ronnie, son of Dr. Harrison and Jean Posey is arrested again in connection to a robbery at a local diner." Henley skims the article and stops dead in her tracks as she reads "the odd thing is the only thing stolen was frozen food from the freezer." Rambling Ronnie just stealing food Henley questions out loud catching herself off guard. No charges were held against Ronnie, as he was only eight at the time, however the next headline is "Dr. Harrison Posey places troubled son in Fairfield Institution as abuse rumors surface." Henley clicks on the article and finds that even at the young age of ten Rambling Ronnie begins spouting abuse claims about the profound Dr. Harrison. It says that the terms for Ronnie would be three years, Henley ponders that is a long time for just a boy.

As she digests these articles and dives deeper into his past, she finds out the drug abuse didn't begin until Ronnie was fifteen, that is many years after all the rumors and the stealing begin. Henley thinking this is peculiar. She decides enough about Ronnie, let's find out more about Freakshow Freddie.

She dives into the search with the first headline of "lost child found at Comet Carnival." Henley scans the article to see a picture of young Freddie with blonde disheveled hair and baby blue eyes. A gloomy image portrayed while he is clutching a brown teddy bear for dear life. She sees the confusion in his eyes, as the article says that the boy has been lost since age two. He has traveled through the states with the carnival. Unfortunately, due to inhumane conditions of the carnival the little boy was locked in a box in the back of the bus.

Hitting the back button on the page, she sees the second headline of "Carnival boy murders a wife and husband. Boy sent to Garrison Detection Center for redemption at just the age of thirteen." Henley felt uncomfortable at the idea of a thirteen-year-old committing a gruesome murder. Henley adjusts herself as she reads on and on about Freakshow Freddie and his claims that he has six personalities. The thought that this little boy murdered a wife and husband before he even was considered a teenager makes her stomach turn.

Henley continues her search as she types in Sally Clayton, the wife of Dr. Johnny Clayton a world-renowned Pediatrician. She becomes consumed in the love story of the two. A romance starting just when they were kids, which turned into high school sweethearts. Sally supported him through his medical school, and even his medical career in the Marines, in which they finally settled down on Hill Shawl Lane. They lived a majestic life together, full of galas, full of luxurious parties, full of award ceremonies, and more specifically full of love. However, tragically their love story came to a screeching halt when Dr. Clayton coming home for their 50th anniversary was struck head on by a drunk driver. The drunk driver survived with no injuries, but sadly Dr. Claytons life was taken on impact. The crash was only a half mile from their home, in which Sally following her nightly running routine found her husband before police even arrived.

Sally was never the same. The man that was her best friend since she was seven years old was gone and she had no one around her. Doctors at first thought it was depression, then heartbreak because other than her mind she was physically well. But as the years progressed, she started living on the streets and wandering around while having conversations with her late husband. Always glancing to her side as if Dr. Clayton was walking beside her himself. This was such a horrific event, no wonder she went crazy, Henley thinking. To find your husband's mangled body trapped inside and not able to do anything would be enough to make anyone go crazy. Henley glancing down at her clock decides to shut her laptop and her brain off as she realizes it is a lot later than she expected.

She gets up and grabs her phone to see a text from Ava. "Hey girl, it's almost time. Are you excited?"

Henley typing back, "Of course, can't wait to see you." She runs downstairs as she is greeted with the smell of her favorite meal. Her mom hastily cooking lasagna for lunch.

Spending the next hour and half talking with Sebastian about the fun events she has planned for the night. She is taking board games, laser tag, and somehow, they will get everyone to play hide and seek in the manor. All of these sound like kid games but in a 10,000 square foot manor how could it not be exciting? The rules around the night include no drinking, no drugs, and no inviting people over that don't have tickets. The town will be locked down as always at 9:00 p.m., so after that they will be locked in the house with no one over the age of nineteen. All bags are checked by the police at the entrance, and everyone is searched before they enter just as a precaution.

The manor will be fully equipped with food and if for any reason they run out of food, there is a cook that lives on the acreage surrounding the manor that is a call away. Henley's dad has been studying the concept of letting her go since she was little. Henley ultimately was surprised when he finally told her two years ago, she could go.

They finish lunch, just as Henley phone lights up with Levi texting that he is only an hour away from picking her up. Henley excuses herself from the table and goes upstairs to get ready. She gets dressed feeling slightly older as she looks in the mirror and sees the dark green shirt peeping through the black leather jacket. She decides to curl her hair as she turns on her curling iron. She finishes her hair and puts the final touch on with her jewelry and her light red lipstick. She grabs her bag full of her overnight clothes, her snacks, and her games as she realizes it is already 2:45 p.m. Levi will be here in fifteen minutes, her heart beating fast as she rushes downstairs.

Her mom and dad look up. She sees her dads' eyes glisten with joy and her mom beam with happiness as they tell her how beautiful she looks. Henley thanking them for a good lunch as says she loves them and puts her bag down by the back door. She slides the back door open and yelling bye to Sebastian.

"See ya later brat. Have fun," Sebastian responds.

Her dad questions her with his normal concerns of do you have your phone, wallet, knife, and charger. Henley calming him down, kisses him and her mom on the cheek as she hears Levi pull up. Excitedly, reaching for the door opening it just in time to see Levi making his way up the sidewalk.

Levi looks at her and she can almost tell he is trying to catch his breath, as he says "Henley, you look amazing."

She smiles as she looks at his outfit consisting of ripped jeans and his blue t-shirt that matches his eyes. Henley feels her heart pounding in her chest just as his Elvis looking curl falls down on his forehead. "You do too!" She exclaims as he takes her bag from her. "Are you ready for this?" he asks.

"Of course, been waiting for a while," she responds, almost unable to contain her excitement.

Ava leans out the back window as she yells, "Come on lovebirds we got 45 minutes to get there," as she winks at Henley.

Henley hops in the front seat, as she automatically reaches for his phone in the console to put on the Halloween playlist, a playlist they took great pride in as they all had made for this trip. He puts her bag in the back, and slides in the driver seat. They listen to ghostly songs from Hocus Pocus to even old Halloween rhymes as they chat about the adventures to come. Tonight, will not only test their friendship, test their character, but ultimately the course of their lives will change forever.

The area that they drive through is on the outskirts of the town with the loveliest views of the mountains and the land that Wyoming has to offer. Given that it is October, covering the area is a range of orange, brown, and red leaves. October has always been Henley's favorite time of the year. The road leading up to the manor is blocked off any other time of the year, so this will be the first time that they have physically seen the manor.

Levi says, "Well guys here we go." as he turns on the long winding road that is covered with a tunnel of Aspen trees overwhelming the evening sky. Ava gasps and snaps a picture; she has always been a sucker for scenery. Henley glancing over at Levi as the scene creates a glow on his eyes and makes her fall deeper for him. But why hadn't he mentioned the kiss? Why hadn't he acted further on it? Henley already overthinking. Maybe tonight, they will be able to get some time alone to further discuss their future and their feelings with one another.

They continue to drive through the tunnel of trees for about 3 miles with no other houses in sight, almost creating a hostile environment.

Finally, Levi anxiously says, "Well there she is."

They all peer out through the windshield at the most gorgeous, obnoxiously large towering home. Daffodils and lilies covering the landscape with a black stone walkway up to a white wraparound porch. On the porch there is already a line of excited young adults waiting to enter.

"You ready?" Levi winks as he asks.

"Let's do this," Ava says from the back. They gather their things up still admiring the large manor with delicate soaring Victorian pillars. They see the black dramatic double doors swing open as they make their way to the line.

A small frail lady in her early 50s walks out "Welcome everyone!" she bellows as she opens her hands in a wide huge motion.

She is followed by a young man no older than 30 with eyes so piercing it sends a chill down Henley's neck. He begins to go over the guidelines while the lady introduces herself as Ms. Hamilton. She takes out a bag asking for all cell phones to be given up.

Ms. Hamilton then turns to the young man and says "This is my son, Jeffery, He will be in the guest house and will be available by phone if anything is needed."

Jeffrey runs through the motions of looking through everyone's bags. Intensely making sure there is nothing in there that is not allowed. They explain that the cooks have prepared a feast but if for any reason food runs out, there will be one cook on the property all night and will be able to be contacted by phone.

Ms. Hamilton then says, "Well kids, this is where we leave you, please enjoy your time on the property and be cautious of your manners."

With that Jeffery and Ms. Hamilton make their way down the stairs to the black paved path as kids run into the front door. Henley watches as they walk off not understanding why the exchange seems so quick and almost as if is rehearsed. Henley carefully watches as the two fade into the distance to see if they will bother looking back.

Unnervingly, and eerie not once do the mother and son glance back at their guests. Henley finding this extremely odd. There are fifteen strangers entering your manor and you don't seem the least bit phased? Henley dismisses this by acknowledging the fact that this happens every year for them. They are merely used to it.

Levi breaks her thoughts "let's go kid, it's time to party."

Levi says, "Woah this is massive," as he walks in looking up at what seems to be 15-foot-high ceilings. Henley is intrigued by the flower arrangements consuming the entry round table, and the side table. The art on the walls looks like something out of a movie with elegant abstract painted scenes of children playing in the fields, dogs running, and memorials of woman in big graceful dresses posing on chairs.

Ava leaves them in the entryway. "Come on dumb and dumber, let's check out the kitchen." As she pushes through a white revolving door.

Levi glances over his shoulder at Henley as he disappears through the door following Ava. Henley placing her bag down on the entry table and following the two, slamming into Levi's back as he is completely frozen looking at the kitchen dining table of ten vintage red and black chairs. The tabletop overwhelmed with decorations of pumpkins, black candlesticks, black table runners, and delicately accented with red and black roses. The type of decorations Henley thinks she will do when she is older. Off to the right they see another white revolving door, they make their way through as it opens up to a brass kitchen with black cabinets and a pearly white island. Welcoming the smell of an immense amount of food. From hamburgers, hot dogs, steaks, chicken, fish, caramel apples, bags of candy, chips, salsa, and any kind of soft drink imaginable.

Henley looking like a kid in a candy shop, "Well I know where we will be the majority of the night." Levi softly pushing Henley's shoulders laughing.

"They weren't kidding when they said we would have food." Ava says.

"You guys let's see the rest of the house before we get too excited." Henley patiently says.

At that moment, Josh and the cheerleader posse come barging in. Just as anticipated, they make some overrated cliché joke about Henley leather jacket while Levi and Josh quickly tell them to shut up and go enjoy the night. The eye roll and death glares are inevitable from them as Henley brushing past them without a glance to make her way through the door.

Henley, Levi and Ava make their way up to the fourth story. Naturally due to their love for movies they navigate to find the closest bedroom to the movie theater. On the fifth story there's a basketball court and a pool. Henley ponders to herself the logic of having this on the top floor does not make sense. Despite the weirdness of the construction, it is overall unique, Henley thinks. They put their stuff down in their rooms and look at the clock. It's only 5:39 p.m., which is way too early for dinner so they decide they are going to go to the third floor and glance around the library. The library is enormous with bookshelves to the ceiling and ladders on each side to climb to the top. Henley isn't really sure why anyone would need this much stuff; it is like an attempt to build a town inside their manor so they never would have to leave.

Levi makes his way through the books, he has always been fascinated with old books like the "Great Gatsby," and "To Kill a Mockingbird." He uses these to disassociate from the real world. Not to mention, the idea that someone can have a unique idea and create a novel that turns into such a classic. Henley, on the other hand, likes thrillers and horror. Ava doesn't read much.

Levi's eyes light up as he goes through the old books. While Ava occupying herself by sliding the ladders up and down the wall, just being her normal goofy self. The three of them waste about an hour and half just rummaging through the library. It is Levi that breaks the trance and decides that he is finally done looking at the books and asks if they want to go watch a movie.

They make their way up to the movie theater and see some of the people getting ready to play nerf guns running past them to go to the fourth floor. Other kids playing hide and seek throughout. The theater is just like the ones on the square with a huge projector and red leather reclining seats. They decide on a classic that they watched growing up, Friday the 13th. A movie that they would thrill themselves on watching every Halloween. It never scared them growing up but being here in this manor Henley must admit it feels eerily different.

The movie finishes around 9:00 p.m. just as the windows and doors steel shutters slides down over them.

"Time for lockdown," Levi mumbles.

Ava beginning to twiddle with her hands, as her nerves take over. Henley recalls the few Halloweens they all spent together as children, and how every time the shutters cover the houses Avas' anxiety would rise. The lockdown is an event that has happened as long as Henley can remember, the kids never were given an explanation other than that is just how it is. They never ask questions; they just know that at 9:00 p.m. on Halloween every year the whole town locks down. The town's decision that all buildings and homes would have iron shutters installed on them and the police department would control the switch to make them go down. If for some reason you weren't in a house or a building, the police would pick you up and take you to the police station to make you wait it out until morning.

Henley remembers Ava telling them how it creates a feeling of her in a trap.

To help alleviate her thoughts Levi chimes up, "Let's go eat then we can play some of the games Hen brought what y'all think?"

Ava says, "I want steak and candy." She hurries out of her seat, as if eager to occupy her mind to something other than she is locked inside.

They make their way downstairs through all of their classmates, with some playing water balloons, with some playing nerf guns, others just laying staring at the ceiling. They go into the kitchen to see that most of the food is still there Henley believes that everyone has too much excitement to eat. They make their plates and sit down to discuss what they should do next. Henley feels a sense of déjà vu creep up which is then accompanied by a frightening feeling.

Chapter Four

Levi

As he sits down with his plate, he can't help but think about the ride with Henley and Ava. Henley looks absolutely stunning; he almost couldn't breathe when he picked her up. It was like the air was completely ripped out of his chest. Her blonde curls on the drive continued to wave in the slight wind from the window being down, a look Levi knows he will never forget. He glances at Henley across the table to see her moving her food slightly around with her fork. She doesn't like her food touching; a little quirk Levi loves about her.

He knows she is patiently waiting for him to explain his feelings further. And he will tonight, he just has to find the right time. She has never looked more beautiful than she does tonight. He knows this night would be a night they will all remember.

He looks at Ava, thinking to himself how she is such a good person even though she has had her fair share of trauma. A trauma he remembers almost destroying her. He will never understand how she overcomes it daily. Her sister's wreck had become the staple of their early teens. Her sister was four years older than them. Levi doesn’t really remember her as he only was ever around her in passing. But he does remember her lively personality. She was always so upbeat. Ava idolized her. He remembers that night that Ava and her family found out. A night where Levi had held Ava crying just as she had done for him years before. That was the night that Levi vowed to be their rock when life hit. It is almost like the three of them can overcome any life event as long as they are together.

Thinking to himself he knows he will always be their rock, even if it is from far away. He never wants to give up that position. These two girls help create the man he is today, and he wouldn’t be who he is without them. As long as they will have him, he will always be around. He sees Ava sling her straw at Henley as they both gleefully laugh together. He knows this night will be a night they would all remember.

Chapter Five

Ava

Sitting across the table, Ava sees Levi keep glancing up from his food to the two of them. Levi will always be her big brother. A big brother she didn't know she needed. The three of them have been through so much from her sister, to Levi's mother, to Henley falling madly in love with Levi. She knows they would make the perfect couple as soon as one of them speaks up.

Ava can see the looks her two best friends are giving each other. She is so ready for them to get together already. She has known Levi loved Henley since they started high school. It was in his eyes. She knew Henley felt the same but didn't want to admit it, she was funny that way.

Ava remembering the drive up to the manor with open fields. Wyoming has always been so beautiful to her. She was ready for high school graduation, their road trip for their last summer, and then rooming with Henley at college. They were always going to stick together, she knows this. They always did. The three of them have always dreamed of going to Yale. A school they idolized since they were little. Henley and Ava would room together and Levi would be their protector at the parties. Ava thinks back to why they picked Yale, and honestly it was probably just because that was the only big school that they remember hearing growing up. Nevertheless, they have stuck to it. All three working immensely hard throughout school, from getting straight A's to always going above and beyond in extracurricular activities. They were bound to get accepted.

Ava knows deep down she is slightly terrified to move away. She loves Wyoming and after she graduates, she will most likely move back to this state. However, she knows that she won't move back to this town just because ever since her sister's death she has wanted nothing more than to leave this town. Her parents had offered for her to move to her aunts in Texas but Henley and Levi are the reason she stayed, she needed to be with them at that time. As she is sitting looking at the two of them, she wonders what her life would have been like if she had left.

Vaguely remembering Texas from when she visited there, her mind takes her back to the tall overpowering Oak trees in open fields. She remembers thinking it was so beautiful as nature has always been something she is intrigued by. But no matter the sadness that this town has brought Ava she loves her life just the way it is.

Chapter Six

Henley

Being in this manor is creating a more dreadful feeling now that lockdown is here. They have no cell phones and no outside communication other than the wired phone on the wall. But honestly, what could happen? She brushes it off because she believes she knows everyone in the manor tonight.

Levi, pushing his steak away, announces "I think I want to get a group and play "Never have I Ever." Ava excitedly agrees, as Levi stands up clapping his hands together "Everyone, let's play Never have I ever," he bellows.

Josh, Tommy, Chelsea chime in from the entryway, "Let's do it!" Heather, Autumn, Destiny all agree surprisingly. Henley is not sure why the cheerleaders want to play other than the fact Josh and Tommy are.

Levi sees Berkley sitting by herself at the far end of the dining room table eating chips and salsa. "You want to play?" Levi asks.

Berkley looking up "sure!" she excitedly answers. Almost like she is surprised she was asked Henley ponders. Which in all fairness they don't really include her much in anything. Berkley only moved here four years ago, and honestly is extremely quiet.

Levi, not missing a beat, "well great, this is going to be so much fun!"

They make their way into the large living room and nestle down by the enormous gray stone fireplace. All sitting around the massive stone coffee table, surprising to no one Josh sits a bottle of Rum down grinning from ear to ear. Henley glances at Levi and Ava as they both know Henley does not drink.

Ava mildly suggests "Guys we can have fun without drinking." This suggestion is followed by eye rolls, and soft groaning.

Levi, trying to soften the room, says "We are playing Never have I ever, we are already going to get into trouble with each other."

The group laughs and agrees as Josh takes the bottle off the table. Chelsea chimes in she is going first and starts off strong with "Never have I ever had sex." Eyes scanning over everyone in anticipation to see who puts down their finger. One by one Henley sees fingers go down that are no surprise to her as she makes her glance to Levi. She slowly sees his finger go down and ultimately her heart drops.

Levi's eyes meet Henley, as she can see them glisten in pain. Henley can feel the crowd turn on her as her shoulders tense and she can feel her hands tighten on the edge of the table. Her body language giving her feelings away. Henley gets up dismissing herself to the kitchen. She vaguely hears Levi mumble "You guys continue playing."

Henley feels her breathe catch folding her arms as she sees Levi makes his way to the foyer. She pushes her back against the demilune hoping to make herself disappear to avoid this conversation. Levi's shoulders slump down almost as if in defeat and his eyebrows are furrowed trying to figure out how to bring this topic up Henley guesses. A look of pure remorse for his actions. He reaches the big round table in the middle of the foyer as he places his palms on the table trying to brace himself and just stares at Henley.

Henley deciding to break the tension and says "So, who is she?" Levi shaking his head and looking at the table as he mumbles "It's not like that."

Henley defiantly saying "that's not what I asked, I asked who is she?"

Finally meeting her eyes, Levi says "It was the summer I went away to my uncles', right after my dad started drinking again. I don't talk to her and it meant nothing."

Henley trying to think back to that summer, a summer she remembers was so difficult for Levi. His dad had broken his sobriety and the two had a huge fight before Levi getting sent to his uncles. She sees Levi squirming nervously as he waits for her to speak. Henley looking at him as she can see his regret, his remorse, and his uneasiness. In that moment Henley decides that it isn't even worth the argument, because to be real they aren't even in a romantic relationship. She ultimately has no reason to be upset. However deep-down Henley can feel the stab of hurt in her heart. She lets her arms fall beside her as she shrugs and chuckles.

She says "well, buddy you are the first of the group."

Henley starts walking to Levi extending her arms, he embraces her as she jumps in his arms and he swings her around holding her tight. Henley knows the hurt feeling is going to linger for a while, however she wouldn't dare let herself be bitter for too long with him. She couldn't, she never could stay mad at him. After a minute or so he finally puts her back on solid ground as she unclasps her hands from around his neck, she feels his breath against her cheek as she leans back to look at him while he still holds on to her waist.

He smiles and says "there is my girl, she's back."

Henley feels her heart skip a beat as she yearns to kiss him. She sees a twinkle in his eyes, as she tries to fight every urge in her body, she can feel herself leaning closer and closer to his lips. She feels her body jerk forward almost as if the universe is pushing them inward. She closes her eyes as she purses her lips to meet his. As their lips touch, Henley can feel her body cave into his arms, as the environment around her goes silent. She can feel his tongue lingering her lips almost as if his body is debating if he should go further. Henley slightly opens her lips just as she hears Ava run in shouting their names.

Henley instantly let go from Levi as Ava giggles and says "It's about time."

Henley straightens up and asks "What's up Ava?"

"Well, the group wants to play hide and seek with all the lights out and everyone puts in some money and the winner gets the pot." Ava says. Levi without missing a beat pulls out his wallet and begins counting his cash.

He hands a $100 dollar bill to Ava and says "This can be for all three of us."

Ava grabs it and skips back to the living room. Henley glancing at Levi as he nervously puts his wallet in his back pocket.

Henley pushes his shoulder and says "We've got to win," as she makes her way to the group.

After counting the pot, Josh announces to the group there is a total of $500 up for the winning. The rules are simple. No one can go into the rooms with the doors closed, the team must stay together and hide in the same spot, and if one person of your team is seen at any point by the seekers your team is then it. They decide it will be easier and fairer if they break up into groups of five with three on each team. Obviously, it is Levi, herself and Ava on team, team 2: Josh, Tommy, and Chelsea and team 3: the cheerleaders, and team 4: consisting of Berkley, James, and Regan, the last team consisting of the outcast group of kids with Collin, Elijah, and Blair.

The leader of the team plays rounds of rock paper scissors to decide who the first lucky seekers are. Which end up being the cheerleaders. Henley silently snickering to herself as she internally contains her excitement. Josh breaks the group as everyone suddenly runs off to find their hiding spots.

Levi, Henley, and Ava scramble up to the 5th floor. They think by the time the cheerleaders make it up there someone else would have surely been caught. They get there just as the cheerleaders' scream "Ready or not, here we come".

Henley hides behind the gymnastics mats on the side of the court, Levi hides in the utility closet beside the mats, and Ava lays underneath the bench almost instantly being consumed as her shirt blending in with the darkness along with her dark hair.

They wait as they hear the cheerleaders going up every floor, opening and slamming doors calling out to get people to come out. This goes on for about 15 to 20 minutes until finally they hear what they think is Autumn screaming out "Got you!" And Tommy's team groans in unison as Josh says, "Okay everyone meet in the living room." They all make their way down laughing at Josh's team. Once gathered in the living room Josh says, "okay round 2 guys, Break!" as everyone rushes off to their spots.

Henley's group plan again is to get to a high floor so they decide on the 4th floor in the movie theater. They scurry up to the 13th row, with the intent that they will hide in the aisle until another team is found. Henley laying down in front of Levi, and Ava laying down at their feet. They can hear Josh shuffling around on the floors below searching as Tommy is saying "Come out, come out" and Chelsea rummaging around the rooms. This goes on for about 30 minutes and then suddenly they hear a scream. Levi and Henley hop up thinking it will be followed by a "Got you!" of some kind. But they are very much mistaken. As it is followed by a thudding sound with Tommy screaming "Who are you?" and is answered by a grunt and a deep man's voice shouting "Someone you know!"

Henley feels chills go through her whole body as Levi incredulously stares at her and Ava, as they hear Tommy screams stop. Did they just hear what they think they did?

Chapter Seven

Levi

Henley and Levi crouch back down next to Ava, as the next few minutes that follow are loud grunts, screams and hastily running feet. Levi minds racing, unable to fathom what they just heard. Surely, it has to be a joke. Levi, calculating the layout of the house, a gift he picked up from following his dad on the job sites, he believes the screams came from the 3rd floor.

Levi can feel the girls' bodies tense up, and he has no idea his next move. If this is serious, how in the hell is he supposed to get them out of this? His emotions and thoughts are cut off by Ava's voice.

Ava shakily says, "Maybe it is a joke, you know, to get everyone to come out."

However, just as she says that they notice that the movement has ceased. Which means Josh, and Chelsea must have made it to a hiding spot, and no one else is leaving theirs.

Levi follows Henley gaze across to the movie screen and sees Berkley, James, and Ragen peeking out from the side. Berkley slowly puts her finger to her mouth in a shushing motion and disappears behind the screen again. Suddenly, Levi can hear a blow of hard deep footsteps coming up the entrance to the movie theater. He feels Henley cringe next to him and sees Ava grab onto Henley's shirt as they see an image of a large man appear in the little fog lights at the bottom of the theater.

Levi bows down lower underneath the chairs trying to catch a glimpse of the person. He sees brown steel toe boots, and black baggy pants that are covered in a liquid substance. Henley gasps as Levi glances over at her in an attempt to distract her, the floor is hit hard with a long wooden pole with a black spiked ball on the end. A weapon that looks like it came directly out of a horror movie. Levi peers closer to see that the spiked ball is covered in red substance. Levi instantly feeling a pit in his stomach as he knows Tommy is not just hiding somewhere.

At that moment Levi feels Henley's body begin to shake tremendously as if it is being taken over by sadness, fear, worry and anxiety all at once. The man makes his way up the stairs slowly stopping at every aisle. At every stop he glances down the aisle waiting to see any type of movement.

Ava whispers, "We have to move you guys."

"Where?" Levi looking at her in disbelief. "Where do you want us to go?" As he is still unsure what the next course of action should be. Almost as if Levi is instructing them Ava slowly slides back on the ground to the other side of the aisle as the man is now on the seventh row and is gaining on them. Levi knows they should start to move, because if not they will be just sitting ducks. Levi motions towards Henley to follow Avas' lead. Levi can hear the man breathing heavier and heavier gaining on their location. With each step that is taken the sound of the spiked ball hitting the floor is overpowering.

Time is running out and Levi realizes they have nowhere to go. He will see our shadows moving and once he gets to the thirteenth aisle there will be no escape. With the same pit in their stomachs and the same incredulous fear in their eyes, the trio realizes they have no idea how to get out of this situation. Just as the man reaches the twelfth aisle, Levi sees Berkley peek her head out of the side of the screen and place up a stop signal. Levi feels Henley clutch his sleeves and whispers "Stop," as Berkley loudly whistles the sound illuminating the outside hallway. The man's head jerks to the side confused as he grunts and hastily runs down the stairs and out the entrance of the room. Levi, Ava and Henley halt in their spot for what feels like a lifetime, holding their breath waiting to make sure he doesn't come back.

They hear him make his way up the 5th floor and aggressively search the basketball court and pool.

Levi decides this is their time, so he stands up and mouths to Berkley "Let's go." They make their way down quietly to the entrance and meet up with Berkley, Ragen and James. The six decide to slowly go down the stairs to the

3rd floor which is the library. It will have more hiding spots until they can find some of the others.

Levi can only imagine that Josh and Chelsea are running back downstairs or found somewhere to hide. From the sounds of it, they were on the third floor. Levis' eyes beaming with a look of fear with and a mixture of confusion.

Chapter Eight

Henley

Henley can feel the anticipation with each step as they tip toe downstairs to the 3rd floor. Berkley's team in front, followed by Henley, Ava, and Levi in the back. Each person continuously peering over their shoulders to make sure the others are still behind. They are about halfway down the stairs when they suddenly hear screams coming from what seems like the living room. Instantly, the two groups stop dead in their tracks with an immense amount of terror running through their veins. Even if they wanted to, they can't move. Henley feels Ava tug on her shirt as the screams state stop and abruptly develop into multiple thuds as someone yells "Round 2!" Henley glancing back to see Ava's eyes starting to fill with tears, and Levi's face in utter shock.

Levi whispers, "Let's go now."

They rush down the remaining steps and run into the library. Levi gently closing the door behind them and locking it as the others scurry off to find a hiding spot. Henley cautiously making an effort to watch where everyone goes as she nestles underneath a vintage chair in the corner of the room. She sees Levi and Ava stay fairly close to her, Levi hiding behind a cabinet, and Ava underneath a desk directly in front of her. Berkley makes her way behind a curtain, James hiding behind a bookshelf, and Ragen goes into a closet beside the bookshelf James is behind.

Henley can feel herself losing her breath, as she is softly gasping from the fear and the horror of the fact that it seems like some of their friends may be seriously injured or even worse dead.

People that she knew, and people that all grew up together could need her help and she is unable to get to them, and the fact they are inevitably stuck inside. The six of them remain in the library for what feels like forever as more screams and thuds occur following with what seems like little catch phrases. So far, they have heard "Someone you know", and 'Round 2". Henley mentally taking note of everything: from the phrases, to what areas she thinks the person is in, the number of thuds that occur, and the depth of the voice each time a phrase is yelled.

She sees Ava looking at her with a wide-eyed gaze. Henley knows Ava is thinking about her sister's death. A death that she remembers shook the town. At the time of her sister's death Ava was just twelve years old. Her sister had gone on a road trip with her friends right before her

Senior year. However, right before they hit the town city limits on their way back their car was found abandoned. The town searched for months, but no one was ever found. For years after, Ava would have nightmares where her sister would be on the back patio trying to get in the house with blood running down her face. Ever since her sister's death, Ava didn't handle eerie situations well. Henley just wants to hug her best friend and tell her it will be all okay.

Henley decides to quietly distract Ava, she softly whispers "Do you remember going to the carnival when we were younger?" Ava just nods her head. "Well, it's just like that, it's just a maze and after that we can stuff our faces with cotton candy."

Ava smiles in reminiscence and mouths "Thank you."

James peeking around the bookshelf says "Guys, I think we are okay to come out," but he is suddenly interrupted as they hear the creak of the floorboard as the doorknob begins to rattle. All their bodies tense as Josh slams back behind the bookshelf and they try to go deeper into their hiding spots. The door swings open and a man with broad shoulders appears in the doorway. Henley can see him clearly, half of his face covered in burn marks with jet black hair almost to his eyes. His hair appeared to be slimy like it hadn't been washed in years. But the thing that makes Henley's stomach churn is the piercing gray eyes.

Henley wraps her arms around her knees pulling them tighter to her body. Despite this being impossible, she instinctively tries to make her body small enough to where she disappears altogether. Henley can feel her breathing getting quicker and quicker as she sees the man step into the library dragging a sword across the ground creating an awful ringing sound. She glances at Ava as she can see the man's shadow overwhelm the desk that she is hiding underneath.

Chapter Nine

Berkley

Berkley realizing how small this room is and how they are ultimately stuck here. She thinks about how quiet it is, so quiet she can hear the breathing of her classmates. From behind the curtain, she can make out the shadows of her classmates' hiding spots. She can also see a shadow standing over what appears to be a desk. Before going behind the curtain, she didn't catch all the peoples' hiding spots. She honestly is only worried about James and making sure she has him in her eye range.

James was her first friend here when she moved, really the only one that even bothered to be nice to her. She remembers how awful it was moving to a new area right before starting high school. She can still feel the anguish she experienced with her parents. Her parents were always gone, so she always wondered why on earth did it matter where they lived. Berkley instinctively knows when she is asked about her parents, her response is they travel for work. But the truth is, yes, they travel for work, but they never come home.

They give her an allowance and pay the bills; and they make sure she has everything she needs. But they never see her. When Berkley was born it was a surprise to these carefree archaeologists who only have one vision in mind, travel the world. Her mom attempted to stay with her the majority of her childhood taking her on their little adventures up until she had to start school. So, at the age of five, Berkley got a nanny. However, when they moved to Rocky River, Wyoming from Los Angeles Berkley had talked her parents into getting rid of the nanny. She has been alone ever since.

She admits it was hard at first, but then she slowly begins to realize she had been doing this her whole life just in a different way. She remembers feeling so alone when she first got here, and she remembers being overwhelmed with how close the community was. It appears on the surface like a barrier that can't be broken from any outsiders, until James introduced himself one day to her while she was drawing underneath the tree in the park. He had complimented her picture; he was the first person to do that in a long time. And after that it was all over, they spent every waking minute together.

As she stands behind the curtain trying to anticipate this looming shadow's next move, she sees James peek out behind the bookshelf near the door to the door that is left wide open. She sees him take a look around the room as her body tenses. She knows him well enough to know his next move. He is going to make a run for it. She wishes she was closer so she could signal for him to stop, but she can't. She begins shaking her head almost robotically in response, even though she knows he can't see her.

Sure, enough just as the big shadow begins to bellow James slender body slides out from behind the bookshelf and casually out the open door behind the man. Berkley feels her body let out a silent sigh of relief, as she follows James' image to where she can no longer make him out.

Chapter Ten

Ava

Ava can feel how close his body is to the desk. Her mind is not sure what to do, and her body is unable to move like it's glued to the hardwood floor. She glances at Henley pleading for an answer or a solution to prevent anything from happening to her and her friends. Ava doesn't want to let her thoughts run wild, but she has an unnerving feeling something bad is going to happen. Something that will forever change her friends.

The man suddenly whispers, 'Do y'all really think I don't know y'all are in here, I can sense y'all."

Ava sees Henley bite her arm in order to prevent a whimper from coming out. Ava then instinctively covers her mouth so she doesn't let a sound out.

The man looks up to the ceiling snickering as he sucks his teeth in, "This will be fun," he declares.

Ava feels a gust of wind in the air as she suddenly hears a slamming on the desk. As hard as she tries to prevent this, Ava can't help but let out a whimper.

He peeks under the desk as he says, "There you are little girl," as he grips Ava by the back of the head making her stand up in front of him.

Ava knows at this moment; this is the event that will change Levi and Henley. She closes her eyes wishing she could make him disappear. She envisions her family on the beach, her sister and her playing in the sand making castles as her parents look at them with glee in their eyes. She realizes at that moment her family will now lose two kids. Their only two kids.

Ava doesn't even want to look at Henley, she doesn't want Henleys' last memory of her to be this. Opening her eyes to see Henley's face with a look of pure terror. Ava wishing this wasn't her end. She has big dreams; dreams she will never get to experience. Dreams of graduating, dreams of college nights with Henley and Levi, dreams of meeting her husband at college, and dreams of walking down the aisle and eventually having kids. She can feel a tear fall down on her cheek. She doesn't dare wipe it away. She wishes there were things she could say to her parents and to her friends. Things that will forever be unspoken now.

She has enough courage to mouth the words "I'm okay," to Henley as she sees Henley eyes glisten. She feels the man tightening his grip on her hair almost as if he is expecting her to kick and try to get free. Ava knows better, she knows this is it for her. Avas' concern is more about how her parents will take it and how Levi and Henley will survive after witnessing it. She sucks in her breath preparing for whatever torture will happen next.

In that moment, Ava feels the rush of the wind as she sees out of her peripheral vision the shiny silver image of a sword swinging to her neck. She shuts her eyes hard, wishing she was somewhere else, a coping mechanism she established after her sister's death. Her mind takes her back to an image of her last family picture with her sister. A time when her life was peaceful and her family life was peaceful. As she feels the cold blade meet her neck, she thinks I get to see my sister again.

Chapter Eleven

Henley

Everything happens so fast; it is hard for Henley to fathom what she is seeing. She sees Levi instinctively run out just as the blade hits Ava's throat. And with that, she sees Levi falling to his knees.

The man snickering as he says, "Well wasn't that fun?"

As Ava body falls to the ground while he continues holding her head in midair. In almost synchronized motions, everyone rushes out of their hiding places darting for the door; some screaming and some crying. Levi, traumatized with fear, stays on his knees Henley jumping out and grabbing his arm. He glances up at her in a petrifying state of shock as she can see goosebumps form on his arms. Looking at his face unable to decide what to do next Henley sees an overwhelming amount of blood on his face. Ava's blood, her best friends' blood. She pulls him towards the door as the man drops Ava's lifeless head to the floor and says, "Don't go, the party is just beginning."

Henley and Levi make it out the door as they look behind them and see Ragen running as a sword comes flying through her chest. Ragens' eyes meet Henleys' one last time as she sees her chest collapse while she takes her last breath and falls to the ground.

Levi, snapping out of his frozen state, grabs Henley and Berkley and yanks them into a closet down the hall. He locks the door behind him. Henley slumps her body in the corner behind the jackets pulling her knees close. Levi anxiously wipes his face on a jacket sleeve, as he looks at Henley.

He kneels down in front of her and says, "We are going to be okay Hen."

Henley can feel her body begin to go limp, her eyes blinking fast as in hopes to wash away what she just saw in her mind. She can feel her hands growing cold as she scrubs her face trying to get the blood to start flowing through her body again. Did she really just witness her best friend die?

Berkley softly sobbing in the other corner says, "Guys, he is right down the hall. He is going to check all the rooms on this floor."

Levi moves the jackets aside and starts feeling the wall.

"What are you doing?" Henley questions.

"Manors like these are bound to have a secret hideaway," he replies.

Henley doesn't dare object but she feels that it is a slight reach to think there is some kind of hideaway.

They hear the man coming down the hall, sliding his sword along the hardwood floor. "Why did y'all run, we were just getting started?"

Berkley suddenly says "Where did James go?"

They all remember seeing James escape prior to Ava's death, but no one knows where he went. Henley a little taken back that this is Berkley's first concern as to what they just witnessed.

Henley, not thinking, snaps back and says "Seriously, after what we just saw that's your first response."

Levi quietly calming them, "Girls, come on we all want to get out of here and we are all concerned for the others."

They hear door by door as the man is opening and slamming them shut as he makes his way through. When suddenly they hear a door swing out and the man yells, "Well, we found one." They hear a man's voice as he begins to grunt and fumbles.

Berkley whispers "That's James."

Before any of them can even attempt to figure out how they can help James, Henley hears the swipe of the sword come down hard as James screaming ceases.

Berkley whimpers as she falls to the ground. Henley kneels down in front of her as if she is a child and grabs her face in her hands and softly says "I'm so sorry, but we have to think of ourselves now. We have to find a way out."

Berkley nodding her head in agreement as Henley helps her to her feet again. Levi urgently trying to find a way out as he rummages through everything in the closet. A crease in the back wall suddenly opens as he presses his body weight against it. Behind the wall it appears to open into another closet.

Levi ushers Berkley in as he looks at Henley. "We have to go," he pleads.

She can hear the man slowly getting closer to their door. She runs in, and Levi follows behind while quietly closes the opening behind them.

Berkley, Levi and Henley all look in disbelief as they are directly in the kitchen now.

"How did we end up here?" Levi asks.

Henley replies, "Does it really matter? We're two stories away from that man now."

Berkley says, "And we are closer to the phone in the entryway to call for help."

Levi, suddenly remembering the phone, rushes into the entryway. They find the phone hanging off the wall with no cord attached.

"Well shit, of course they killed the phone." Levi angrily snaps.

Henley looking down the hall to the living room suddenly sees four bodies sprawling out on the couch, floor and in the fireplace. Henley gasping as this catches Berkley and Levis' attention. They both turn and look in horror. After moments of standing and staring at them in shock, Henley sees a small photo on the ground by the table.

She sluggishly makes her way to the living room ignoring all of Levis' attempts to stop her. She reaches the photo and picks it up to see a young boy holding a teddy bear with disheveled blonde hair.

"Rambling Ronnie is here," she says gasping for her breath. She shakenly holds the photo out to Levi as he rushes over to her.

"What's this?" he asks as he flips it over to read "If you can guess why we kill, you will be able to leave at dawn."

Henley behind her tear-stained eyes can only make out the words Rambling Ronnie wrote as she begins to realize this is a game. Berkley looking around the scene in dismay to see Josh, Tommy, Chelsea and Autumns' mangled bodies all over. Chelsea continuously burning in the fireplace, and the others all lying face down on the furniture with bloody gashes in their backs and heads.

"You guys, can we move to another room please?" Berkley asks.

"Yeah, let's stay moving." Henley grabs the picture and shoves it in her back pocket as they make their way to the 2nd floor.

Chapter Twelve

Levi

They make it to the 2nd floor and can tell that the most of the rooms are bedrooms. They see one room off the side that has multiple arcade games as well as a massive TV and couch. Levi meticulously shuts the door and locks it behind them. They sit on the couch to breathe for a minute. Levi thinking back to how quickly Henley figured out the picture of Rambling Ronnie. A person he hasn't thought of since they were kids.

Touching Henleys' arm next to him he says "Hen, how did you know that picture was Rambling Ronnie?"

He sees Berkley lean forward from beside him looking in Henleys' direction.

Henley begins speaking by saying "Guys, I have been noticing Old Man Jones wandering around town with a group of other people."

Levi says "Well that is not uncommon, he comes out every October."

Henley says "Yes, but the people he has been with every time I see him, I didn't recognize so I looked it up. I found out some weird things about Rambling Ronnie."

As Henley goes over Rambling Ronnie's story: from who his parents are, to his drug usage, to his abuse rumors and then ultimately being placed in Fairfield Institution by his own parents. Levi remembers vaguely hearing all this in passing when they were kids, and he always wondered what happened to Ronnie.

Levi asks "So, he is here?"

Henley nodding her head continues with pulling out the picture from her back pocket and says "Yes, this is a picture of him as a little boy."

Berkely sighs as she says "Well this is great; we have a crazy man looking for revenge because no one believed him."

They sit there in silence for a couple minutes, all of them contemplating their next move. The silence is broken by Levi finally speaking.

"You guys, I have to get to the guesthouse, Jason will be there."

"You can't go," Henley says.

Berkley suggesting, "it is our best bet."

"How? We can't even get out the doors or the windows," Henley interjects.

"I forgot about that!" Lev slamming his fist against the wall.

"We just have to play their game and figure out the clues. They will let us go at dawn," Berkley mumbles.

Henley suggesting, "Or we could just wait until the walls come up and make a run for it."

"Are you insane?" Levi questions.

Berkley stating "there is no way they will keep us alive until then, we have to play their game. It's our only option."

After some deliberation, Levi agrees. "So, we have to go to the floors where our friends were murdered," Levi asked incredulously.

"I guess so." Henley says.

"Well, we better get going, it is already almost 3:00 a.m. Doors will open at 7:00 a.m.," Berkley points out.

Henley goes through the events out loud, just hoping she remembers them correctly. The floors that the murders have occurred on include the living room, the 5th, and the 3rd. Given that they have already gathered the clue from the living room, they only need to go to the two other floors. They decide to make it up to the 3rd floor which ultimately will be the hardest for them. Henley isn't prepared mentally or emotionally to face that scene again. And she hadn't even begun to think about how they were going to explain everything if they make it out.

Levi leads them out of the arcade room and down the hall to the stairs. He can feel the uneasiness from Henley and Berkley as they are very cautiously following behind. Henley holding onto Berkley's hand behind her. It feels like an eternity before they reach the stairs even though they were only a few feet away. They tiptoe up the stairs, each one holding their breath with every move they make. Once they reach the top stair all of them at once sigh out in relief.

Levi turns to face Henley. "If you want, I can go scan the room for clues so you don't have to see anything?"

"No, that's okay," Henley says.

Levi knows she is just trying to convince him that she is okay. Levi sees Berkley tugging at Henleys' hand as they shoot each other a look of reassurance to move forward.

Levi faces the library as he begins to feel tears swell in his eyes. He feels a warm familiar hand grab his as they all stand side by side not wanting to enter the room. Once they enter, they will forever envision the horror once more. All three are silently afraid that the gore will begin embedding in their minds. They walk into the doorway as Levi drops Henleys' hand and goes directly to the spot where Ava's body is lying. He turns to see her head a few steps away.

He sees out of the corner of his eyes, Henley falling to her knees. He goes to her side making an effort to block Ava's body from her vision.

'Come on Hen, let's make this fast." Levi says.

"We've known Ava since we were three, and now she is gone." She cries with desperation in her voice.

"I know, but we have to get out of here and tell her story. And we can't do that if we break now," Levi pleads.

Berkley interrupting the conversation, 'You guys, that teddy bear looks extremely misplaced."

Levi standing up and walking to the teddy bear sitting on the chair that Henley was hiding underneath originally. The bear is missing an eye, and the arms have a look of scorching as if someone took a torch to them. The fur being eerily matted with dried blood. Blood that looks like it has been there for years.

Levi quickly turns to Henley and says "let me see that picture you had."

As she hands him the picture, he instantly sees the teddy bear in the photo with the same missing eye. It is another clue to Rambling Ronnie and his past. But was he the one in both the living room and the one on the third floor? Also, who is the guy that was in the movie theater? Levi's mind racing with these questions just as they hear noises coming from the floor beneath them.

Levi hurriedly grabbing Henley and Berkley as he rushes them out of the library into the bathroom on the same floor. He locks the door behind, all of them silently hoping that whoever is making that sound is not an enemy. Henley and Berkley crawl inside the cabinets underneath the sink as Levi closes the cabinet doors behind them softly saying he will be in the shower.

The sounds filling the walls like echoes mimic the sounds of a carnival happening. Levi trying to put his thoughts together over the deafening carnival music. What is the significance of this music, and why the hell does it sound like there is a party going on outside he thinks to himself.

As he stands, there in the shower, he begins to remember the stories they told as little kids. If this is Rambling Ronnie, then the others here have to have some association with the other stories they told as kids. His brain keeps going back to Henley mentioning that Old Man Jones was with a group. A group of who though, he remembers Rambling Ronnie scary stories, Old Man Jones scary stories, and vaguely someone named Sally and Freddie. But for the life of him he can't remember their stories.

Chapter Thirteen

Henley

Henley begins to steady her breath as she feels Berkley touching her side. She can hear carnival music blaring as she gets an uneasiness about being so far from Levi. Suddenly she hears cries start out. As the cries begin to ring louder and louder overpowering the carnival music. The horrific cries she believes belongs to Heather and Destiny. Berkley squirms closer to Henley, as the cries suddenly turn to screams following sounds of blowing hits.

These unbearable sounds go on for a little bit, making Henley's stomach churn with every sound. However, just as fast as it started, the screams and the crying subside. The eerie silence takes over the environment. Just when Henley thinks whatever nightmare that could be is over, the silence is consumed with a loud and bellowing "And that Ladies and Gents is the show!" with a whipping sound.

Almost like a rope hitting the hardwood floors Henley thinks. They hear the person retreat down the stairs assumingly to the 1st floor and hear clattering in the kitchen as if they are eating. Levi peers back the shower curtain as Henley softly cracks the cabinet door open.

Levi delicately says, "Let's make our way to the 5th floor now." Henley can only nod as she opens the door further and he steps out of the shower.

They unlock the bathroom door and gently open the door as Levi gazes around the corner. He gives the all-clear signal as he guides the girls down the hall to the stairs. They step on the steps one by one, with shallow breaths, stopping and listening to every creak or movement in the house. They finally make it to the 4th floor as Levi tells them to stay on the stairs as he goes up to make sure the coast is clear. After about five minutes or so Levi comes back up the stairs leading to the 5th floor just as they hear a loud clutter downstairs.

They pause in their places hoping that no one is coming. Eventually they reach the conclusion that whoever is in the kitchen is banging dishes together and is merely making themselves a meal. A meal after a murder, Henley shuddering at her own thoughts. Levi exhales heavily and continues on. They finally make it to the 5th floor and follow the same routine of Levi going to check things out before they enter.

Levi comes back and says, "We can go but try not to look around, and keep your eyes on my feet."

Henley nodding as she and him both know neither of them will listen. Levi clutches Henley's hand and pulls her forward just as Berkley grabs her other hand to follow. They make their way down the court and see Collin face down on the court with a ball shaped wound in the back of his head. Berkley grips Henley's arm as she softly sobs. They must have been close, Henley thinks.

Henley's mind wandering back to a time when the school was consumed with a rumor that Berkley and Collin liked each other. Oh, what she would give to just go back to a time when gossip and high school were her only problems. She knows deep down this night will alter her forever.

They continue to walk through the mangled corpses of their classmates as they see Elijah's body bent between two gymnastics mats. His blue swollen face almost unidentifiable sticking out. It appears as if he was killed before being rolled up in the mats. The mats consuming his body like an anaconda with their prey. They make their way across the court as they come to the beginning of the pool. Levi looks down and gasps as Henley and Berkley follow his gaze trying to comprehend what they are seeing. There in the pool is Blair's cut up body with parts floating all over. Henley can't take it anymore and throws up behind her. Who would do this to us? Her and her peers are so young. Who would want to torture individuals who had their whole life ahead of them? The three lock eyes with one another unable to comprehend or even move.

Berkley is the first to make a move as she raises her finger and points across the pool to a banner that says, "You came for mine; I came for yours." Levi walks to the side of the pool and makes his way to the sign, he tugs it down and places it in his back pocket. Henley, still frozen in place, feels Berkley tug on her arm.

"Henley, we have to go to the 2nd floor now." Her mind is overwhelming with thoughts; however, she can feel her body take over and begin to gradually move. They meet Levi at the end of the pool, and for the first time she truly looks at him. She sees that tears have been streaming down his face and his bright blue eyes are a crisp dark blue. She instinctively hugs him, a gesture she has done so many times before, but this time they both know it feels so different.

Henley looks down at her watch to see that it is 5:30 a.m., they don't have much longer until the panels open at 7:00 a.m. Without a word they make their way down to the 2nd floor, with every inch they walk, with every creak they hear, and with every breath they take with such precaution. In hopes the three killers they know of won't see them or find them. Deep down they still hold the hope that this is all a bad dream, a hope that maybe if they are silent enough someone will come out and say it is a terrible big joke. But that is only a hope, they each know that with every passing minute their lives keep changing and they are unable to stop it.

Chapter Fourteen

Berkley

Levi leads the way, now carrying a baseball bat they found in the gym.

Following behind him Henley and Berkley are keeping their bodies so close to his. Berkley deciding to let Henley be in the middle as she feels Henley would want to be close to Levi. Berkley can feel Henley's heartbeat in her hands as they walk in a follow the leader motion. Berkley feels how cold her own hands are, as she knows it is from her own fear radiating down. Berkley catching a glimpse of Henley's eyes she can see the fear and the tiredness weighing in them. It seems with everything happening, neither of the three have had time to cope let alone feel the pain from losing their friends. People they have known for years.

Berkley appreciates the fact that Levi is constantly checking over his shoulder at the girls to make sure they are okay. All of them lost in their own thoughts and emotions as they make it down to the second floor. Berkley could breathe a sigh of relief as she realizes they reach the floor without any more surprises. They all know that they were about to enter the 2nd floor and it is the scene where the worst sounds came from. Berkley tightening her grip on Henley's hand realizing how much she wishes this night would just be over.

Berkley thinking back to how James had begged her to submit her name, she didn't even want to come to this party. But she had caved because she also didn't want to be left alone on Halloween night, she never envisioned that they would get picked.

They reach the stairs to the 2nd floor and Berkley sees Levi sigh heavily almost like he is preparing himself for what he is about to witness. Berkley can feel a lump in her throat, not a lump of sadness' but a lump of genuine dread.

Berkley catching herself counting the steps one by one trying to anticipate how entering that room will feel. She knows that most of her friends are dead and never coming back, but that sadness she feels is being taken over by the fear. Fear that her veins keep pumping out throughout her body. She can see that Levi truly wants to make sure they are safe. She has known of Henley, Levi, and Ava ever since she moved to town. The inseparable trio, the friendship everyone wishes they have. She couldn't imagine the amount of pain seeing Ava die like that. She has always heard the rumors of Levi being in love with Henley; however, she never knew if it was true until tonight. Just by the genuine concern he has in his eyes when he looks at Henley, Berkley just knows. Berkely wonders if their relationship will change because of this night. Berkley sees the regret, a feeling that she knows well that he carries for not letting it come out sooner than now.

Berkley in utter astonishment as her eyes wander the room while her heart begins thumping louder and louder. She hears a creaking above her head as she looks up and her eyes meet her worst fear. She sees her best friend, her only friend hanging from the ceiling swaying back and forth on a white rope. She feels her body give out on her as she falls to the ground. Thinking to herself that this couldn't be real, this couldn't be happening to her.

Her thoughts swarming with all the memories she has with James as they come flooding her mind. Him teaching her how to drive a car, their pizza nights together, him teaching her how to be a teen rather than adult. Times she will never get back and things she will never get to experience with him. How could this be it for them? Why did this have to be it for them? She feels her chest collapsing, she feels her breath become unsteady, and her hands go cold. Here comes the panic attack, the attacks started years ago when she moved here but James always coached her through them. She begins to steady her breath just as she realizes James is wearing his blue jean jacket.

A blue jean jacket she loves so dearly now has blood splatters all over it. His blood, an eerie thought that makes her shudder. This blue jean jacket that he let her borrow so many times before. A jacket she has clung to in the hall, a jacket that always made her feel safe. How can a jacket that held so much safety for her in the past represent a feeling of so much sadness and fear now Berkley thinks to herself. She can't even comprehend the amount of suffering he went through in his last moments.

The room is in utter silence in Berkley's mind, almost as if she is having a terrible nightmare that is mute. She does not feel as if she is in her body. She doesn't believe she is really here. She hugs her chest to her knees sobbing. She hears footsteps coming up to her from behind, but she doesn't even care to look to see if she is safe. She feels a soft hand on her shoulder, as she looks up to meet Levi's eyes.

Chapter Fifteen

Henley

Henley finally gathering up enough courage to take her eyes off of Levi. She glances around the room to see what she can only imagine is a horror movie.

They recognize the friends they have already seen in the other rooms hanging one by one from a white rope attaching to the ceiling.

Henley can't move her eyes off of Ava's decapitated head hanging and swinging from the fan. Ava, her best friend, a girl she has known since she was three. Her friend is never going to live out her dreams or reach her goals. Why? All because of some sick sadistic group of people whose only goal is to torment them. This is completely unfathomable, Henley thinks. A cold sensation rushing all over her body as she lets her tears finally drop out of her eyes and down her cheeks. After everything that has happened that night, Henley no longer can hold back her anguish.

Henley's mind flooding with every time she hugged Ava, every time they held hands crossing a street as little kids, every time they played games outside as little kids, and their dreams for the future. She could feel her crying turn into sobbing as she looked at her best friend. As she stands there, she thinks about Ava's family. A family she loves dearly, how on earth is she supposed to tell them of the horrors that have occurred tonight. How can she even begin to honor her best friend?

Feeling her tears fall, Henley snaps out of her thoughts and finally looks around the room. She sees Heather, a girl she fought with so much growing up sitting straight up on the couch. With a carnival sledgehammer piercing through her throat and her eyes wide open. Henley, so nauseous at the scene, sitting down to prevent herself from passing out. She looks to the corner and finds Blair, a girl she didn't know much about but always knew she was so sweet. Such a sweet girl just sitting there with her back against the wall cross legged. Her head leaning back with a glass bottle slammed down her mouth her throat with a ball inside it. Just like those carnival games, Henley thinks.

She sees Levi walking around slowly out the corner of her eye. She follows his body motions as she sees him picking up Berkley by the shoulders and telling her to not look behind her. Henley eyes darting to what is behind Berkley. Destiny's body on the floor. Her body lifeless on the floor with a tic-tac-toe board carving in her chest. Wooden Os hung around her throat and the Xs covering her eyes. Henley can feel the lump in her throat begin to form, she can feel her stomach churning. She can see the vomit coming out of her mouth as she is hunched over gagging. But, in her mind she is absolutely numb from her body's motions.

Chapter Sixteen

Levi

Levi's mind suddenly understanding the importance of getting the girls out of the room. Having a hold of Berkley by the shoulders he looks over to see Henley in the corner hunching over. He sternly calls out to Henley as she turns to look at him, he sees the tears streaming down her face. Her eyes full of disgust, anguish, sadness, and hatred for whoever did this. A look of almost defeat, a look Levi will remember most of his life.

Levi grabbing both girls, leads them out, and shuts the door behind them. Berkley sobs, fighting Levi trying to go back in, whispering a jean jacket over and over again. Levi trying to calm her as Henley slides down the wall and pulls her knees to her chest.

"We have to get the clue," she stutters, as Levi and Berkley look at her.

Levi says, "Hen, I checked the whole room, there is nothing in there that could be a clue."

"It has to be," Berkley stammering, "we have to find them all."

"Let's check the other three bedrooms," Levi says.

Levi suggests this because he knows neither of the girls can take any more surprises.

Henley says "You go without me."

"I'll stay here with her," Berkley says, slouching down next to her. Levi secretly happy about the fact the girls want to stay behind but also the going alone is just as terrifying.

"Okay, I promise I will be back" he says looking at Henley.

Her soft green eyes a shade he has never seen before, but a shade that if that is the last thing he ever sees he will be content. He kisses her on the forehead as he grabs his bat. He searches the room to the right, finding nothing of significance.

He peeks out the door making sure the girls haven't moved as he crosses over to the second bedroom. He sees banners covering the walls all written in red marker. Red cursive handwriting in the phrases "Someone you know", "Round 2", and "You came for mine; I came for yours" with the final phrase "And that Ladies and Gents is the show!" His mind racing back over the course of that night as he recalls the phrases that the killers were yelling throughout his friends' murders. These have to be significant.

He sees little polaroid pictures between the banners. The environment creating a strange feeling as he sees little stuffed animals sitting everywhere. Any other time Levi would find this terribly creepy, but considering the circumstances this is the least of his concerns. He examines the ground trying to piece together what he thinks can be clues. When he sees two newspaper clippings with headlines of "Carnival boy murdered a wife and husband, is sent to Garrison Institution for redemption at just the age of thirteen" and "Dr. Harrison Posey places troubled son in Fairfield Institution as abuse rumors surface." Levi scans the clippings for any clues. Looking down he sees a toy 69 mustang car. A car he loves so dearly sitting on top of a magazine with a man's face on it that read "Psychologist breaks the therapy world with new breakthroughs."

Levi, unsure why these headlines hold any significance, decides that it is time to bring in the girls. He doesn't want them to be here but ultimately, he would rather have them in a safe room with him than outside by themselves.

Levi peeking around at the girls and whispering, "you two may want to come in."

Levi sees Henley inhale heavily as he knows this is a coping mechanism she created for herself when she is nervous. Levi gives Henley a reassuring nod that the room is okay to enter. Henley and Berkley grab hands saying "Let's do this," as they begin walking to Levi. Levi guiding them through the door as he closes it behind him. He glances down at his watch realizing they have just about an hour left to figure this out.

Levi says "As much as I don't want y'all in here, I need you two and we are running out of time."

Chapter Seventeen

Berkley

Once in the room, Berkley softly says, "Wow, this is a lot to figure out."

Berkley thinking back throughout the night as she remembers hearing all the phrases after one of their peers were brutally murdered. She hadn't thought much of them at the time but as she sees the room with all kinds of evidence, she begins to understand this night has been planned. Most likely it is something that was planned for a while. Berkley feels her body shudder as can't believe how people could plan such a horrific crime. Berkley glancing around the room trying to take everything in that is covering the floor and the walls. The newspaper clippings covering the ground consuming the carpet below. Each wall there is a banner hanging from side to side with red writing on it. Berkley quickly dismissing the idea that the red writing is someone's blood. The corners of the room hold little trinkets from stuffed animals, to toy cars, and to polaroid pictures.

As she picks up a stuffed animal an eerie feeling consumes her body. Looking at this teddy bear her mind wonders if it is from the killer's childhood or from one of their victims. She suddenly drops it at this thought as she turns to see Henley and Levi rummaging through newspaper clippings.

Berkley makes her way to Levi and Henley, peering over Levis' shoulders as he hands some of the clippings to Henley.

Henley, fumbling to find her words says ""“I've seen these before online when I was researching the old stories that we use to tell each other."

Berkley questioning "Why were you researching old stories?"

Henley went into detail about how she felt uncomfortable seeing Old Man Jones around town this month. Him being with a group of people begin to increase her curiosity. She explains the horrible lives of the people they use to make fun of when they were younger. Berkley vaguely remembers sitting around bonfires her freshman year and listening to these creepy stories of the by passers of this town. She remembers hearing of Old Man Jones and his weird family disappearance. But as much as she tries, she doesn't remember the other people.

Berkley says "I really only remember Old Man Jones."

Levi stating "I remember something about a wreck and a wealthy man passing, and something about a little boy being in a carnival. But they were just stories."

Henley says "That is what is weird, most of them are somewhat true."

Berkley says "Well we don't have very much time, so let's each take a wall and look for clues."

They dive into the clues, one by one. Berkley looking at the banners on the wall in red paint, "Someone you know", "Round 2", and "You came for mine; I came for yours," and with the last phrase "And that Ladies and Gents is the show!"

"Those are the phrases that they have been saying after they kill," Berkley declares.

"So that means we are dealing with four different people," Levi utters.

That idea sends a chill down all of their spines. Berkley's mind wondering about all the rooms they have seen someone in. As she explains to Levi and Henley that the rooms all portrayed a different manner of death.

"The 5th floor being the most gruesome, the 3rd floor occurring with a guy with a sword and a burned face, the 4th floor being a guy with a spiked ball weapon, and then the 2nd floor portraying a carnival scene" Berkley affirms.

Levi hands Henley the toy mustang, and the magazine. Berkley sees Henley eyes widen as her shoulders slump in what looks like defeat.

Henley tells them "Y'all need to sit down, I think I know who the people are that are doing this."

Levi and Berkley exchange glances as they sit down on the floor as Henley paces back and forth talking fast with her hands.

She hastily goes through Old Man Jones and how he told her that night she gave him the dessert, "You help me make my decision." How he was a psychologist on the break of greatness when all of a sudden, his three kids and wife disappears and that he only comes out in October.

She clutches the magazine and says this is "Old Man Jones."

Berkley taking in all the information begins to think back to the times that Old Man Jones was the topic of the stories. The stories focusing around the disappearance of his family but also how much the police department really didn't do a full investigation. The police reaching the assumption that it was his fault.

Berkley breaks the silence and says "Someone you know."

Henley asking, "What?"

Berkley explains that she remembers the stories and how the police department never had any suspects for their disappearance. Old Man Jones being very adamant that someone in the town was the reason and that he wasn't the cause but no one would listen.

Levi breaks in suddenly saying "He is trying to tell us that he didn't kill his family, someone else did. But no one believes him after all these years so he finally went crazy. He is in turn killing kids on the night that his kids disappeared because ultimately that is what the police blames him for."

"Okay, great one down. Three to go." Berkley ponders.

Berkley, thinking out loud, says, "Well, this newspaper article talks about Freakshow Freddie from Comet Carnival. So that has to be the man who hung up everyone." She finishes as she shivers.

"So, we have Old Man Jones, and Freakshow Freddie," Levi says.

"But why is he killing?" Berkley questions.

"Well, he has multiple personalities, and was tortured as a kid in a carnival dungeon. So, I guess he just enjoys inflicting pain on others." Levi chimes in, "And he picks kids, because that is when his life changed. I think his saying has to be 'And that Ladies and Gents is the show!"

Chapter Eighteen

Henley

Henley looks down at the 69' toy mustang trying to rationalize with herself as she remembers reading that Sad Eyed Sally's husband drove a mustang.

"So, Sad eye Sally has to be here too." Henley whispers.

"Why?" Berkley inquires.

"Well, her husband was involved in a car wreck and their 69' mustang was totaled. They had been together since they were kids. When he died, her whole life was over." Henley declares.

Levi says, "She is doing this all because she lost her true love?"

"No, Henley says, she is doing this because the person who killed her husband was a drunk driver on Halloween.

A night where kids are supposed to drink and party, just like Josh was."

They all shudder at the name of their peer that just not three hours ago was playing a game with them is now hanging from a white rope.

Berkley attempting to put the pieces together, "What if, the drunk driver is someone's parent that is here tonight?"

Almost instinctively the three look at each other as Levi says "if that is the case, then the phrase 'You came for mine; I came for yours' makes sense."

Henley doesn't want to think about Ava, or the man with the burned face.

But as she is looking down at the paper titled "Dr. Harrison Posey places troubled son in Fairfield Institution as abuse rumors surface." It finally clicks. The burned man is Rambling Ronnie and his phrase is "Round 2!" This is the man responsible for her best friend's gruesome murder. She can barely get it out as she whispers his name.

Levi asks, "But why?"

"Well, no one believed him about his parents," Berkley says, "You see I don't think he was just some messed up kid. I remember hearing about him and the horrible things his parents did. They intentionally burned his face, and then they used his back as their own personal chopping board. But since they were rich his allegations didn't stand a chance in the community. He kills because that is the only time he feels in control." She finishes stating and looks up at Henley.

Henley glancing down at her watch realizing they have very little time left before the shutters come up and they believe they know who the strangers are. She breathes a sigh of relief allowing herself to believe that they have a fighting chance to make it out of here.

Levi saying in defeat, “Well what now? Do we wait?”

They are broken off by the sound of multiple weapons sliding on the first floor and whistling as someone says “Whoever is alive, come down.”

Chapter Nineteen

Levi

Levi, Berkley, and Henley all exchange glances as if their thoughts seem to be spoken through their looks. None of them wanting to move, none of them wanting to face the people who slaughtered their friends. It is a pure distinct feeling of not knowing what to do.

"We have to go guys," Levi says, breaking the silence.

Berkley shivering and Henley feeling like she is about to have an anxiety attack. Levi seizes all the clues from Henley, looking deeply into her hazel eyes, which are such a pure form of green now.

Levi reassuringly stating, "Whatever happens, Hen, please know I got you." He shoves the clues in his back pocket as he turns to make his way out the door.

Berkley shrugs as she looks at Henley. "I guess this is it, we have to go."

Levi following up says "Well according to them, we will survive if we guess them right. And with the way the night is panning out I don't see us having a fighting chance in hiding."

Levi sees Berkley extend her hand out to Henley. Henley reaches out and flashes a simple reassuring look, a look of everything will be okay.

Levi making his way to the hall as he feels the walls meet his shoulders as he leans against for support. Almost as an attempt to brace himself as he looks up and meets the girls' eyes.

Henley and Berkley slowly walk out the door to see Levi waiting for them against the wall trying to hide his emotions on his face. He knows his face is showing a sign of defeat and a sign of being terrified. Downstairs they hear the four people whistling and singing almost as if they were children playing with their friends.

Levi feels a pit grow in his stomach as he thinks to himself how they can be so easy going and happy. How can someone do what they did and be okay?

Interrupting his thoughts is a man yelling, "Come on kids, I know someone is still alive. If you run, it will be a lot worse."

A night that Levi had hopes to be one of the best nights of their high school career turned into a nightmarish unimaginable fright scene. The last three drag their feet slowly down the stairs.

Anticipating every step, every creak, every fear, and every urge in their body to run away. Levi could feel the sweat falling down his neck, he could feel the girls so close behind breathing on his neck. He truly has no idea how he was going to keep them safe, but he knows he has too. Levi knows that once they hit the bottom step, he will do whatever he has to make sure the girls at least get out.

Surely this is a joke, he keeps thinking. But he couldn't rationalize the bodies. His friends' bodies, he couldn't see how that could be a joke. If it was and he prays so hard it is, it is a cruel, disgusting joke. Levi knows deep down if they make it out of this, he will never be the same. But in reality, he truly thinks there is no way in hell they are going to live. He couldn't say that though, he can't let Berkley and Henley feel that from him. Secretly, Levi has already accepted the idea that this is the end. At least it is for him. If these people could torture and slaughter his friends, there is no way they will let three of them live without a fight. A fight that he is willing to die for to get them out.

Here they are, the last step, the step that could alter the course of their lives tremendously. They aren't ready and they all realize that, but the choice isn't theirs anymore. Berkley and Henley exchange glances one last time, Henley tugs at Levi's shirt a thing she has done so many times before but this time Levi feels that it is different. It will be different forever.

Chapter Twenty

Henley

She could feel Levi's body heat radiating, and knows him well enough to know that this only happens when he is truly terrified. In a sense, she is glad she isn't the only one that finds this horrifying. But the other half of her knows Levi never gets scared. She thinks back to all the times he would protect her, like when she broke her leg and he had to carry her for miles, like when Ava's sister died and he had to be the shoulder, and even when he got into his car wreck. Not one time did he ever show any fear. The idea that Levi, her rock, is truly terrified chills her to her core. Justifying her fear.

The same man's voice bellows, "I can hear y'all at the step, you all might as well join the party. You don't have anywhere else to go."

They walk into the entry way. The same entry that gave Henley so much joy less than 24 hours ago. An entry way that she thought she wanted one identical to when she was older. Now the mere thought of seeing these paintings makes her want to vomit.

Berkley and Henley remain frozen in place, they can't seem to make themselves move forward. But as Levi disappears around the corner, Henley knows at that moment she must go. She has to make sure she can always see him, especially after everything tonight. She walks forward without hesitation, merely because the fact she doesn't want him to be alone. Pulling Berkley with her. She feels Berkley half-heartedly trail behind. Berkley motions slowly following suit to Levi and Henley. Henley can feel Berkley's sluggish state almost as if half of her body is telling her to run away. However, Henley is fully confident that Berkley will never leave Levi and her there alone. They walk through the door and to their surprise they just see Levi standing at the round table in the middle with no one around.

"Where do we go now?" Henley whispers.

"I suppose we need to go to the living room." Levi suggests.

They all turn facing the entrance to the living room. They can make out a small fire crackling in the distance with a very little light illuminating from it. Just the mere concept creating an unnerving feeling. A feeling that Henleys body has become accustom to tonight. A feeling she prays she never has to feel again if they make it out. Berkley nudging Levi almost as if to say let's get this over with.

Henley whispers, "Come on Le, we don't have a choice."

He glances at her, his soft blue eyes beaming into hers. A look she's never seen before, a look she now relates to fear.

Together in unison with their hands interlocking, they walk into the living room. As they enter, a small weight that they have been carrying throughout the night feels as if it is lifting off of each of their shoulders. This is not due to the fact that this is the end but due to the fact that they know that they can face whatever is awaiting them. This night instilling a strongness in them that they never had before. Anticipating this moment since the beginning of the deaths of their friends, now it is here. Now they can really understand how the night will end, the night that was supposed to be theirs. Now, here they are, three children who became adults tonight facing a group of people who have made their lives hell while playing out their worst fears.

Chapter Twenty-One

Berkley

Berkley quickly evaluating the room, trying to take in everything in hopes she can create a mental escape plan. To her right she sees an older frail lady with soft gray hair in a bun that appears no younger than 65. She is sitting in the recliner in front of the door gazing into the fire as the flames crackle. A man about 6'7 possibly in his late 40s standing at the end of the couch holding a glass that Berkley assumes is whiskey. She turns to see the burned man staring at the bookshelf in the corner as if he hadn't seen a book in years. Finally, she sees a man leaning on the mantle staring at the fire as his hands are clutching a vanilla folder that has what looks like papers with mugshots of all their friends.

The man slowly turning his face away from the fire while he says, "Well, glad you all could finally join us." His voice sends a bolt down Berkley's body, a voice that sounds so rugged but so tired at the same time. His face shows a look of exhaustion, a look of hopelessness, and a look of insecurity. A face that looks so young but his expressions seem so ancient.

"So have y'all figured us out yet?" he asks quizzically. Glancing between the three of them, waiting for his answers.

It is almost like all three of them lost their voices, none of them could find the words to mutter. Levi, the man of many words, couldn't even begin to make a sound. Henley looking as if her chest was trying to catch up with her breathing. Berkley completely numb from the night just gawking at the fire. Secretly hoping that it would catch fire so they could run.

Berkley thinking back to how fire used to calm her. The sound of crackling and the heat radiating from it always created a peaceful vibe for her when she was growing up. But in this moment, all she wants is it to explode on these people. People who have made their last night of teenage years so unbearable and unimaginable. Berkley never hoping someone so much physical pain as she is wishing upon these four individuals standing in front of her.

The room completely silent, as the four killers standing in front of them are looking at them in disbelief. Almost as if they are in shock that Berkley, Levi, and Henley can't find the words.

After what seems like forever, Levi musters up enough courage to stutter, "We have a general idea."

With that statement the burned man in the corner lets out a slight giggle. "Well, who said that will be enough, kid?" he says amusingly.

"That's enough, let him speak!" The frail lady says from the reclining chair shooting a hell some glare at him from across the room.

"You may continue Levi," the whiskey man says, raising his glass to them. Berkley shivers at the thought that they know their names.

Chapter Twenty-Two

Levi

Levi catching the fact that the man knows his name. A man he doesn't even know. A jolt of shock runs through his body as he realizes they have been studying everyone in the manor.

He finally signs heavily, as he continues, "Where would you like me to start?"

"Start with me," the frail old lady specifies as she stands up grabbing on the cane to her right. She walks up directly to Levi inches away glaring between the three of them, just waiting. Levi suddenly losing all his courage as he is face to face with a killer. Her eyes overwhelming his body, eyes that seem to be staring directly into his soul. Slowly picking him apart from the inside out. Henley identifies the hesitation and fear in his eyes. She can feel his heartbeat through his fingertips, Levi thanking his lucky stars as she decides to interject.

"You are Sally Clayton," Henley says.

With just the mere sound of the name, Levi sees a slight tear appear in the frail lady's eyes. Almost as if she has not heard the sound of her own name in years.

"Well little girl, do you wish to continue?" she whispers.

Levi seeing Henleys chest as she inhales a deep breath and spills out the Sad Eyed Sally story.

"Your husband, and your lifelong partner was involved in a car wreck while driving your 69 mustang. The mustang was totaled and you found your husband's mangled body upon arrival at the scene. A scene you can never get out of your mind. When he died, you lost your will to live, and with that you shut off the world." Henley declares.

Levi can see the lady's eyes go from sadness to hatred with every word that Henley brushes over. Levi can feel the fear of continuing as Henley grips his hand tighter.

Henley mumbling the last bit of the information, "The cause of your husbands' wreck was a drunk driver, a drunk driver whose kid is here tonight. You came for us tonight to make them feel your pain. You kill to show others your pain. And your saying is "You came for mine; I came for yours."

Sad Eyed Sally hums, stepping back as if she is unsure how to respond.

"Damn, girl you are good," she says with a devilish grin. "Well, on what floor did I kill?" she requests.

Henley without hesitation knowing they have at least one right finishes with, "you killed on the 5th floor."

Sally Clayton smiles. "Y'all can live on my end, congrats you guessed it. It is now my time to leave."

And with that Sad Eyed Sally turns to the others and bids them farewell. The frail old lady disappears out the door directly behind her recliner without any reluctance. A door that shouldn't be opened yet. Henley, Berkley, and Levi all glancing at each other because the panels hadn't yet been lifted from the manor. How in the hell did she just exit? Did the killers have a way to unlock some of the panels, and if so which ones and how. Their minds consuming with curiosity but in reality, they couldn't care less just as long as she didn't torture them anymore. Or come back.

"Well, I'll be damned they got one right." The burned face man stating as he sucks his teeth making almost a hissing sound.

The man looking intently into the fire turns around slowly and faces them. The flames magnifying his gray eyes. Levi can feel a sting of hatred along with a terrifying chill run down his body. It is almost as if this killer could see the fear in their eyes. The fear creating some sort of a pleasure for him as he slowly smirks, grasping the folder in his hand.

How could he get pleasure from their fear?

Chapter Twenty-Three

Henley

"Seems like you remember me too girl? Well, you got to save my story for the end," he snickered, meeting her eyes. Henley in that moment realizes that he is ultimately the ringleader. He is the master manipulator behind this creation.

"Since that is the case, I want to get out of here or do more killing, so what is my story?" The burned man faces them quickly with his sword in his hand. The sword completely clean from all the blood from the night. It is so quiet that Henley and Levi's gasp for their breath is so evident. How in the hell is she going to be able to speak to the man who brutally murdered her best friend? She can't muster up the courage to even breathe let alone make a sound. Hell, she couldn't even breathe let alone talk.

Neither Levi or Henley could find their voices, as if their bodies were stunned in place. Here he is the man who suddenly changed the whole course of their lives. A man who has taken their sweet caring best friend from them. All the dreams they had together, all their memories abruptly wiped. Their whole childhood being taken away from them so fast and in such a gruesome way. Berkley could see and feel the struggle they were having. Henly so thankful as she hears Berkley voice start to explain who this terrible man is.

"Your Ronnie Posey, the son of the wealthy Posey family," Berkley whispers.

Rambling Ronnie shooting a death glare with the sound of his own name. A name it appears as if he wants to forget, a name he no longer associates with.

"Go on," he hisses in a slithering tone.

Berkley breathing in deeply as she utters, "Well your catchphrase is "Round 2!" and your weapon of choice is a sword. This is because your father and mother used it as their weapon when you were a child on your back. They would cut into your body as punishment for speaking the truth on them. Your attempts to warn people when you were younger were unsuccessful. No one believed you, and no one wanted to help you. Your family's façade and money are ultimately why the community didn't believe your story on why your face looks the way it does. You kill because it is the only time you feel in control of your own life. The only time that people will listen to you," Berkley finishes exhaustingly.

At the end of her statements, Henley expects Ronnie to go crazy. She anticipates that he will start swinging his sword around with anguish. But, he doesn't. He simply nods their direction, smiles and shakes Old Man Jones' hand and he leaves without any words. Without any acknowledgment that he is ultimately responsible for how these three individuals perceive life now. The same way Sally left. Without any apology.

The man holding the whiskey glass, softly turns around chiming in "looks like you three have done your homework, y'all must really want to live. But y'all can't really think we will let you off that easily, do you?"

Henley, Levi and Berkley all look at each other, exchanging the same thought. They know it is too easy. The knowledge that these tortuous killers could not let them merely go, especially after everything the three has seen.

The man starts off with "Henley, the daughter of the famous judge and the criminal prosecutor. Younger brother is Sebastian. You love Halloween, and have big dreams of being a child psychologist. You love Levi deeply, and always have.

Henley can feel Levi flash a quick glance to her at the mention of the word love.

"Levi, you are a rebel, you love fast cars, big trucks, but your true safe place is in the mountains. You live with only your dad and have no siblings. You take pride in protecting others, especially Henley."

Chapter Twenty-Four

Berkley

Berkley can't seem to keep her eyes off the door that Side Eyed Sally left from. Her anticipation grows wilder with each word these killers say. Berkley feels her body grow cold with the idea that these people are not going to let them out no matter how much they guess correctly. Why should they believe killers? Her thoughts saying stay conflicting with her body wanting to run. She has no idea how with how they should proceed.

As she sees the man sneer as he gets Henley and Levis' lives correct she begins to imagine how long they have been watching everyone. How did they know all this information already? She understands the town is small but they were just kids.

Just kids who ultimately haven't done anything wrong to these people. She sees the man's body turn to face the fire and without being able to control her body she feels her feet take off directly for the door behind the recliner. She feels her feet jump on the recliner seat attempting to hop over the head of the recliner as her hands reach the door knob. She hears Henley and Levi scream her name and just as she reaches the knob she feels a sharp pain on her head. Her body is swung around to face the man as he is snickering holding her hair.

Berkley feeling the instant regret in her attempt as she is staring directly in the murderers' eyes inches away from her face. He shoves her body back in line where she is beside Levi again. She looks at Levi as she whispers "sorry." Thinking to herself how in the hell could she leave these two. The two people who made sure she was safe throughout the night. She knows that if they get out, she will spend the rest of her life indebted to them. Levi touches her arm in show of understanding.

The man sneering at the three of them continues with the statements as he stares at Berkley.

"Now, there is Berkley, the odd one, the one that just happened to appear in this group by accident or luck tonight. You love to draw but have dreams of being an artist. You live alone and haven't had family since you were thirteen but no one knows that."

Berkley squirms at the thought that they now know her secret of living alone. He smiles crookedly as if he feels like he did a good job.

Levi, to everyone's surprise, says, "Well, let me tell you what I know about you now.

You are Freddie Hanson. The boy from Comet Carnival with multiple personalities. The boy who escaped years of dungeon torture physically but mentally his mind did not make it out. You inflict pain on others because your mind is gone. You don't know how to handle your emotions, and these things were done to you so you do them to others. And your phrase is 'And that Ladies and Gents is the show!" Levi finishes crossing his arms.

Freddie takes one look around the room as he downs his whiskey and slams the glass on the mantle.

"Kids, I wish you the best of luck in the future, but I will tell you something if you make it out physically, you will never be the same mentally. That is my ultimate goal in this." And with that he turns and walks out the same way the others went.

Chapter Twenty-Five

Levi

The man with the vanilla folder slowly turns to face them. "Seems you three have run off my friends," he says with a sneer.

Levi gently squeezing Henley's hand, as he feels Berkley tense up and squeeze his other hand.

"Sir, with all due respect, you killed our friends." Berkley hisses.

He chuckles in response with a deep laugh. "You, my dear, are going to go places. So, let's end this before raising the panels, who am I?"

Levi swallows deeply as he begins, "You are Derek Jones, a well-known psychologist. A man who loves his family dearly. However drastically and tragically your family has been taken from you. Your three kids were found dead on this very night years ago. Your wife disappearing shortly after your kids murder and no one has ever heard from her again." Levi musters up the courage to look directly in this man's eyes as he continues. "For years after your children's death in attempt to clear your name you begin investigating. However, no one would listen. People begin to not come to your business, which ultimately led to the closure of your practice. A practice that gave you immense joy. You love helping people. But who wants to listen to someone who couldn't control his own home life? With this you spend years and years locking yourself away, and only come out during October. Partly in hopes that you will catch your children's killer, but that yearning to solve the crime has begun to disappear throughout the years. You have in turn grown cold, and now you kill to show the townspeople that your children's death is not something the town can brush away. "Your phrase is "Someone you know."

Old Man Jones inhales deeply, "Seems like you kids are right however, you are forgetting one thing. You see my wife didn't run off, she has her own family now and has changed her name. Since she was never around for the kids, well no one really knows her that well so looks wise it doesn't matter. So, Levi sir, what do you know about your mother?"

Levi's eyes widening with astonishment as he tries to muster out the words "What do you mean? I live with my father."

Old Man Jones chuckling, "yes right, where is your mom?"

Levi feels tears instantly in his eyes, just at the mention of his mom. He stammers "She's in California. She ran off when I was a kid."

Old Man Jones smiling an evil chilling grin as he puts the vanilla folder in the fire. "Yes, young sir, that my boy is my ex-wife."

This mere statement creates a whole new atmosphere in the room. With a gloomy presence over the room, it is now filling up with more unanswered questions. Old Man Jones crossing his arms, as they stand in a state of bewilderment.

His eyes meet Levi's as he continues, "You see, after my kids' bodies were found, the affair of my wife begin to unravel. Although, the affair had been going on for years, things begin to come out. Like the fact there was a boy that was the same age as our kids. That boy is you."

With that statement, Levi can feel his body tense up as he tightly grips Henley's hand. With almost an unbearable amount of strength. Levi begins to feel the heat rising to his face.

Everyone knows not to bring up his mother. A scar that Levi has not yet come to terms with. Here is a man telling him that he not only has siblings, but he has siblings that have been murdered. His mind racing with so many questions as he can't even begin to fathom what is going on. He just feels anger.

Old Man Jones cutting the silence with a knife softly continuing, "She would come visit you as a child, and wouldn't stay for very long do you remember?" Old Man Jones' eyes narrowing as he questions Levi's memory.

Levi's tears fall down his cheeks. His mind flashing back to the last time he saw his mother. A time he pushes deep down in hopes he will never have to relive it. The moment where she had held his little face in her hands with tears smearing her makeup as she told him this was the last time she was coming back and to not ask questions. Levi can remember the feeling as just a seven-year-old watching her car drive off in the rain, his mind unable to fathom why he couldn't ask questions. Well, here is why. His mother's past, and now her future wherever that is.

Sobbing, Levi says, "Yes sir, I remember."

Old Man Jones affirming "and let me guess the visits stopped around your first-grade year, correct?" Levi, trying to find the words, merely nodding.

Levi has so many questions running through his mind that all he gets out is "Did my mom kill my siblings?"

Old Man Jones eyes glisten in pain as he just stares at Levi.

Levi angrily dropping Henleys' and Berkley's' hands as he yells "did my mom kill my siblings, is that why she left?"

Without answering Old Man Jones looks down at his watch. "Well kids it has been fun, but let me tell you the rules before the panels come up."

Old Man Jones pacing back and forth begins to tell the three of them the next steps as follows:

1. You must understand no one will believe that four adults spent the night killing children and then magically disappearing.

2. You must never speak of who we are, and if you do well not to sound cliché, we will torture your families.

3. This night is changing your lives forever.

4. You must tell authorities you don't know who did this, and you hid the entire night until the adults came.

5. The rooms surrounding this night are clean and there is no evidence of us remaining.

6. Lastly, never come up to us in the town.

He finishes these rules smiling and nodding as he says "You three should be proud of yourselves. I truly am sorry this torture. I am sorry that we had to do this in order to make the town see that no one is safe from harm, even precious kids." His voice breaks as the word kids come out of his mouth. "But it is what it is," He continues.

With that Old Man Jones struts out the same way everyone else went. Henley watches as he leaves into the darkness. Levi slowly falling to his knees. Berkley begins to continuously chant, "It is over." Without further hesitation Henley turns to Levi picking up what feels like his lifeless body to a standing form and drags him into the nearest closet tugging Berkley along behind.

"We have to wait here until others show up, we have to follow his rules," Henley says.

Berkley says, "We must never talk about this to anyone or ever again."

Henley softly touching Levi's shoulders. "Do you understand?"

"I got it," he snaps.

Levi can feel the blood in his face and his rage boiling all over his body.

It seems like forever until they hear the panels come up, and even a longer time until they hear Jason and his mother come in the manor. They hear Jason scanning the rooms and finding the corpses as the only evidence of this frightful night. They hear their blood-curdling screams with each passing moment.

"Is anyone still here?" Jason begins calling out.

Almost as if that is their queue that it is finally okay to come out. Henley opens the door and calls out "We are in here."

Chapter Twenty-Six

Henley

Jason and his mother come running to the sound of their voices. The mother and son are greeted with tears covering Henleys' face, Levi in utter shock with Avas' blood smearing his face and Berkley's whole body shaking.

The next few moments are a blur as she can't seem to make out the words coming out of Jeffrey's mouth. But she sees his horror and disbelief as he tries to reassure them it will be okay or something along those lines as he ushers them outside. His mother covering their sides, so they don't see the gruesome scene. Henley thinking to herself as nice as this gesture is they have already witnessed everything. Scenes that Henley can only describe as a living hell.

Henley can feel the warmth of the sunrise welcoming them, a feeling she thought she might never feel again. Just as cop cars are speeding down the drive, she sees Berkley in the light and can tell not only is she shaking but black mascara is covering her face. Henley glances at Levi to her right to see swollen eyes from crying and her friends' blood on his neck and chin.

The cops begin ushering them to the back of an ambulance. The crowd bombarding them with the normal questions when a tragic event happens such as "Are you hurt? "Is this blood yours?", and "Do you have any wounds?" Henley thinking to herself she will take answering their questions all day long in comparison to having to answer her parents' questions. Her brain unable to fathom what in the world the trio will say once the police begin interrogating them. The EMTS do their due diligence to make sure they are physically okay, and provide each of them with a blanket to wrap around their shoulders as they wait for their families.

Henley sees the cops rushing to them as Berkley grabs her hand. A gesture in itself that seems so small, however after tonight this has almost become a safety net for them. Henley glances at Levi as if to say stick to the story, but to her surprise he is staring straight ahead showing no emotion. Henley knows at that moment Levi's carefree and rugged personality will forever disappear. As she stares at the man, she loves a gut feeling consumers her and she suspects from now on he will become distant and cold. Just like the gaze she sees now.

The cops separate them one by one and ask the grilling questions of "Who did this," "Where are they", "What did you see", and "is one of you or all of you responsible?" Henley, Berkley, and Levi all sticking to the story Old Man Jones created. Henley is completely aware that the cops can distinguish that they are lying. The story in itself that these three young individuals hid while they were hearing the gruesome murders in the background is fully unreasonable. The cops know they didn't just hide the entire night while their friends were slaughtered but other than the bodies there is no evidence of who is responsible. And in reality, it would be as if they all made this up if it weren't for their deceased peers.

The three of them wait, not wanting to accept the fact that they are about to have to face not only their parents but also the parents of their friends. One by one, almost as if they are in a horror movie, they begin to see their friends' bodies as the coroners transport them out with a white sheet covering them. The cops tallying the bodies and adding them to a piece of paper in their hands. Henley thinks to herself, that piece of paper has Ava's name on it. A name that means so much to her, but for the medical professionals it is just another mark on their paper.

Her thoughts are broken by Sebastian running up screaming her name with her mom and dad rushing behind. He hugs her hard almost as if he is surprised to see her. Quickly realizing that she could be hurt, he leans back and double checks to make sure he didn't break her. Her parents spout a million questions as they check her to make sure she is fine. She sees Levi's dad running up to hug him as well. She knows that Levi's relationship with him will change but she feels that it will become stronger just based on the news from Old Man Jones.

Henley can see Levi's shoulders untense as he embraces his dad.

She glances over at Berkley and quickly realizes that something is off. Berkley lives alone. Surely, she has parents that would still come. But there is no one running to her, there is no one checking her body for the slightest scratch. Berkley turning to face Henley as she says, “Berk, you, okay?”

Berkley deflecting, “I’m fine.”

“Mom, Dad can Berkley come home with us?” Henley asking.

“Of course, she can,” her dad blunts out without a second thought.

Henley and Berkley hug Levi goodbye as they all go their separate ways for the day. As they get in the car, Henley glances back at Levi to see him walking away with his shoulders slumping down and his eyes facing the ground. She knows the pain he is going through and plans on calling him later this evening. But something feels off, something about the way he is leaving makes Henley feel that their friendship is strained.

Chapter Twenty-Seven

Old Man Jones

Off in the distance, Old Man Jones is quietly watching the events unfold as he hides behind the pillars. He can see the defeat in the trio, and the fear in their parents' eyes. A feeling he knows well, a look that he remembers giving the same cops when he was given the news of his own children. He sees Levis' dad hug him, just as he saw him do many times before. Levi always will hold a special place in his heart. Old Man Jones having some type of attachment to him.

Levi's guess was correct, as he thinks back to his ex-wife and her mental health. She always wanted to have the perfect family. So much that any type of falter in her ideology would create unbearable anxiety in her. Old Man Jones remembers the first time he saw this side of his wife, he remembers feeling scared for himself and their children. But never did he think that one secret, a secret of a little boy could alter his life so much.

He remembers first hearing about Levi. His wife coming inside their house and sitting him down as she tells him that Levi began asking questions and she was leaving the town to never return. Her explanation that while visiting Levi just as she normally did, he began asking questions about her life. As she left to go pick up his kids, something in her mind switched and she took out her anger on his sweet precious children. Old Man Jones remembers how badly he wanted her to die, he remembers lunging at her across the table but to his surprise he felt the sharp knife in his shoulder. His wife not even giving him an apology while watching him stumble back as she slowly turned away from him and walked out.

Old Man Jones had searched high and low for her and without prevail he decided to take matters into his own hands. As he sees Levi's dad drive off with him, he watches Henley and Berkley glance back at the manor before slamming their car door shut. Secretly he hates the man he has become, but he knows deep down the town will not only learn from this but will take the necessary precautions to prevent this from happening again. With that he solemnly picks his briefcase off the ground and slowly turning his back on the creation that changes the town.

Chapter Twenty-Eight

Henley

The way home is silent, but Berkley and Henley are both still clutching each other's hand as they gaze out the windows. The same scenery that felt so warm and peaceful before now feels like a horror story. A scenic view that she loves, as well as her love for Halloween has become just a scarring memory. They make it home and reluctantly climb out of the backseat.

Her dad, shaken by everything, reassuringly says, "I am so glad you girls are okay."

"Thanks, Dad." Henley composes herself enough to get those little words out.

But what her parents don't realize is that they are not okay, and they won't be for a while. If ever. Her parents try to refrain from bombarding her after the horrific accident, but Henley knows they all have questions. Who knows, maybe in due time the truth will unfold but not by either three of them.

Her parents with so much good intention in mind they know the girls need to eat. Henley and Berkley stomach churns as they try to push down at least a little food. Her parents do a double check over their physical bodies to make sure nothing is off. Relieved, Henley and Berkley finally make it up to Henley's bedroom. Henley quietly shutting the door as she slides down the wall so happy to see a familiar environment. They sit in silence for a few short moments as they try to collect themselves. Henley breaks the silence in the room by stating that they need to at least shower. She lets Berkley take a shower first, as she wants to decompress on her bed and reach out to Levi.

She decides to call Levi. His familiar voice greeting her as it reaches voicemail. She decides not to leave a voicemail but instead sends a quick text.

"Thank you for everything. I love you, and I am here when you want to talk."

Berkley comes out of the bathroom. "It is all yours," she says as she sits on the end of Henley's bed. Henley gets up gathering her things, as Berkley says in defeat, "Thank you for letting me come here."

"Of course, girl, we are all going to stick together now, you can stay however long you want or need." Henley hugs her feeling like Berkley can finally relax.

Henley lets the hot water roll down her back, showers have always been Henley's escape. Tonight, it will also be an escape but also a bittersweet moment. A moment of solitude, a moment of isolation, a moment to allow herself to cry, a moment to reminisce on all her memories with Ava, and a moment to mourn her classmates.

Her mind is still unable to comprehend the night's events. As she thinks about all her peers who lost their lives that night a thought crosses her mind that she is unable to prepare herself for. She wouldn't see Ava tomorrow. As she lets the hot water roll down her back, she feels the sobs coming on. She feels the panic start to set in her stomach. How is she going to spend the rest of her life without her best friend? As she falls to the shower floor, she cradles her legs to her chest as she feels water streaming over her. She just sits for a minute.

She can see the steam in the air as she knows it is time to get out, time to get up and face the music. She washes what she feels is blood out of her hair. Henley vowing to herself that after she leaves this bathroom, she will not let this event rule her life. Although she will never understand why, she knows she can't speak about it to anyone. At least those are the rules.

Chapter Twenty-Nine

Berkley

Berkley spends the time Henley is in the shower to silently distress and shut her brain off for a moment. Glancing around the room she sees photos plastered on a bulletin board of Ava, Henley and Levi. From Ava and Henley lighting fireworks to Levi throwing Henley in the lake as Ava is laughing in the background. Berkley has always wanted friends like that, friends she can count on. She only had one good friend. And he is gone now. She feels the tears slowly falling; she knows she will be sad for a very long time. But just like everything else bad in the world she will have to find the strength to push forward. Push forward and live her life. As much as that night was miserable and horrific, it help create a friendship with Henley. A friendship she feels will be unlike any other.

After what seems like forever, Berkley sees Henley come out of the bathroom. With her eyes bloodshot, her face puffy, and with her hair in a towel. She knows the pain she is experienced in that shower, because she did the exact same thing. She knows that whatever emotions Henley has about that night have been washed down the drain with her pain. They didn't say much as the two crawl into bed, even though it is the middle of the day, their bodies and mind beyond exhaustion.

Berkley sees Henley checking her phone one last time to make sure Levi hadn't called, Berkley knows that it hadn't gone off while she was in the shower. Although Berkley didn't know Levi that much, she thinks maybe they all need a little space after their experiences in the Jefferson Manor.

Berkley softly whispering "Goodnight, Hen."

Henley taps her hand and responds, "goodnight girl."

Chapter Thirty

Levi

Levi can't even begin to fathom what to do next as he sits on the edge of his bed. His father was kind enough to not ask any questions, and gave him his space. But he truly didn't know what to do next. He knows he needs to shower; he knows he needs sleep; he knows he needs to respond to Henley. But he just sits. It is almost like he can't move. His mind racing back and forth to what Old Man Jones said about his mother. If he is telling the truth Levi will never truly know. He cannot and will not bring this to his father. Because if he does, it will not only spark questions but it will also break the rules that Old Man Jones had laid out for them. He can't even talk about it. He knows this will ultimately affect his life, and he knows that Henley and him will never be the same.

Levi sitting there for a while and contemplating what to say to Henley, and for the first time in his life he has no idea. Does he apologize for not being able to save Ava, does he tell her he loves her and nothing will ever change that, does he promise to always be there, or does he just remain silent. He chooses the latter, because right now no words could express what he is feeling. He sits his phone on his nightstand, but he doesn't understand the magnitude of his silence. He doesn't understand that in that moment he changes everything.

As the next month's fly by, the trio meets daily at the police station as they spend their time with cops interrogating them still. Levi has spent so much time in that building that he knows most everyone on a first name basis. No matter how many times he is questioned and no matter who asks him Levi sticks to the story. The story that Old Man Jones had instilled in their minds that night.

Levi only sees the girls in passing as he is to report to the police department everyday just as they are. Henley the first couple of weeks would steal glances at him, but after a while he begins noticing her stopping. However, he will always glance at her. He will never stop looking at her when she isn't paying attention. He hates the way their relationship begins to fizzle out, and he secretly doesn't know why. Yes, she had texted and called him multiple times but time is all he needed He had assumed eventually he would reach out but he never found the courage nor the right words to say. So, he just never did. Half expecting, one day she would just show up on his doorstep, but she hasn't yet.

Mentally he is so tired of staying at home and answering the same questions over and over again, he feels his best bet is to just go quiet. His dad pressing, and the cops pressing for more information. But he will not budge. There is no point in reliving the same story over and over, especially when the results will never change. He had gone back to school quickly, almost a month after that night. He remembers hearing that Berkley and Henley were only going to come back three months before graduation. So, he was secretly preparing himself to pass them in the halls. And he knows that Monday will be the day they return. Two more days and they will be done with their daily meetings at the police department and finally they could move past this

Chapter Thirty-One

Henley

Now sitting at graduation Henley thinking back to that fateful night. That fateful night everything changed in her life. She hadn't talked to Levi in over six months, because he never took the time to respond. A cut that hurt Henley's heart so badly. She had spent weeks trying to get a hold of him, eventually she gave up. Why was she trying when he stopped? And when they were all ready to go back to school, he never bothered to pick her up again. But regardless, the time she has spent with her family and the bond with Berkley helps her keep her sanity. Henley just received her acceptance into Princeton, and Berkley on her way to the University of California for her Art. She had heard through passing that Levi had got accepted into Yale. A boy she once knew who had every dream and ambition under the stars, she is so unsure what his goals are now.

Glancing over at his spot among the rows of students graduating, his beautiful once short Elvis hair had become so long. A look that Henley never could envision for him. His body still slumping over, she flashes back to the day she saw him walk away from her. A day that in her heart she would forever hold onto. This was the day she had felt the disconnect between them, a disconnect that they would never be the same old Henley and Levi. Henley longs in her heart a day where she could call upon her old friend once again. But secretly, Henley didn't think that day would ever come again. That fateful Halloween night changed everything. Even the town itself.

The town becoming so obsessed with the murders and what happened that night, that they have completely petitioned to shut down Halloween for years to come. Cops now patrol every neighborhood at night, and the parents are way stricter on kids. Almost every parent instructed their kids to be inside right at 4 pm. Right before the sun begins to set. Parents are now in a fight and flight mode. Some standing ground for a few months after trying to fight the idea everything should stay the same. Others taking flight mode and either leaving town completely or basically locking their family inside. Everyone began to suffer and the carefree attitude of the town was gone. Of course, no one was ever charged or ever questioned. Unsurprisingly, as the three of them are the only ones that even know the truth.

They had been interrogated again and again, but they all stuck to the original story. After gruesomely long months of daily interrogating and investigating the cops finally accepting that these kids were not breaking. In all honesty, they kind of became outsiders to the community. The remainder of their high school career had been miserable. Levi isolated himself, and Berkley and Henley became each other's only friends. Sometimes Henley wishes that she could just hug Levi again and ask him why. But she knows, he wouldn't be able to give her an answer she liked or even wanted to hear.

Chapter Thirty-Two

Berkley

Berkley so nervous to leave this town but also thinking it is very exciting. She could finally go somewhere no one knows her story. No one seeing her as the survivor. She is so grateful she had Henley these last few months, without her it would have been hell. They never talked about anything that happened with words, but their looks to each other said it all. Berkley enjoying the nights she spent with Henley's family. She loves the games nights and the dinners together. Berkley now knows what a real family is like.

They both are so happy to be leaving. Making promises to each other to visit very often at each other's schools. They both know that they will very seldom come back home, not even for the summers. They lost the feeling of home that night. This place became a horror movie to them, not a home.

Berkley sitting at graduation with her mind wondering what California will be like. Looking forward to the scenery she knows it will be a lot different than Wyoming. When she applied there honestly that is all she wanted, was something different. The landscape and open fields just remind her of fear now. She wanted an area that was so crowded that things like Halloween could not happen.

She wants to feel safe again, a feeling she lost that night. As she looks around the crowd, she sees parents surrounding the area when their child's name is called, she sees them clapping in joy of their accomplishments and she suddenly feels a longing for her parents. A feeling she hasn't felt in some time. Her parents had called her the next day regarding the Halloween nightmare, she remembers the conversation being brief and to the point. Not once did they mention coming home, Berkley didn't expect they would. She remembers hanging up with them and seeing the look in Henley's face, a look of sorrow. She remembers Henley quickly trying to change the subject and get her out of the house.

Somewhat she expected it to change things eventually like she half expected them to be here today, but of course that wasn't the case.

Chapter Thirty-Three

Levi

Levi hating how much time had passed and he hadn't checked on Henley or Berkley. But he couldn't, he didn't know what to say or even do. He knows deep down he will always love Henley. But he has to do it from a distance. His heart is so full of anguish and regret from that night. A night he couldn't stop the horrors from happening, a night that he couldn't protect for Henley. She didn't know that he had anticipated the day she decided to come back to school. From that first day she came back he would sit outside the school in the mornings every day to just make sure Berkley and Henley made it there safely. Or that fact he picked his phone up so many times to send her a text but couldn't. But he was going to Yale to study criminal justice and become a homicide detective. A decision to pursue this in hopes of preventing any other young adult from having to experience the horror he went through. He knows deep down he is forever going to be chasing the ghost of Ava, as well as his inability to protect Henley emotionally that night.

Halloween is meant to be a night that is meant for children to enjoy scary movies and candy. A night Henley would never enjoy the same way. He intended to fix that; he didn't know how but he would.

The trio lost in their thoughts, all reminiscing back to that fateful night. All thinking about the fact that in just a few short moments they will collectively feel as if the burden of Halloween will be lifted. As the valedictorian finishes up their speech, they begin thanking everyone and their families for coming. The trio begins to believe they had made it out of here without any mention of that night, just as she mentions the three lone survivors. In unison they slightly bow their heads down almost in hopes that no one will pick them out of the crowd. Their fellow classmates begin to cheer and holler as a hand of applause is followed. Levi, Henley and Berkley all feel the uneasiness as the eyes wonder to their backs. They have spent the remaining of their high school career trying to outrun that night.

The months preceding graduation have been consumed with the trio trying to reach some state of normalcy among their classmates. However, it had been greeted with such defeat. With every room any of the three walked into they were filled with looks, and some even clapped when they entered. They each wanted this day to be merely about graduating. But of course, the last thing the Senior Class and the crowd will remember is that Levi, Henley, and Berkley had survived a night that so many didn't. A night that inevitably made them heroes. And with that memory embedded in the towns minds they are instructed to stand up and throw their caps into the sky. A sentimental moment that was considered as one last hooray for the Senior Class.

Henley, Levi and Berkley all standing in unison with their fellow classmates as they wait to proceed with tradition of releasing their caps into the sky. A moment the trio has waited for their entire existence. But somehow it feels different than the three had anticipated. They will never understand the amount of loss they had that night. It wasn't merely they lost their closest friends, but they lost their innocence. An innocence the trio would yearn for their entire adulthood. Unfortunately, their fellow graduates as well as the crowd doesn't seem to take notice of the sullen loss as they are expected to follow suit by releasing their caps.

Levi throwing his cap in the air; however, he cannot shake the feeling of joy stinging with a feeling of deep remorse. A remorse for losing not only Ava, but also Henley. He realizes as soon as they leave today, that loss of his two best friends will forever represent a hole in his heart. How can he be so happy and gleeful to leave this town? A town he swore he would never leave, a town he saw Henley and him getting married and raising kids in. How can so much change just by one night? A night he wishes everyday he could change, one little change in that night could have altered the course that his life is going. Oh, how he wishes he could take everything back, how he wishes he could have talked Henley and Ava out of going. They could have easily created their own Halloween sleepover. As he watches his cap fly down to the ground, feeling his heart sink to his stomach as he accepts the fact he cannot go back now. He has to move forward, and he has to find contempt with it.

Chapter Thirty-Four

Henley

A flood of emotions consumes Henley. She is unsure how to feel however she knows that whatever she is feeling is okay. To her surprise, Henley is welcomed with a sense of relief. A relief that her story here is finally over. That she is able to leave this town and never look back. She never has to relive that night, nor does she have to be remembered for it every time she enters a room.

They made it, they truly made it. As the caps fall to the ground and people leave their seats to meet their families for pictures, the trio can't help but seek one another out in the moving crowd. Levi, Berkley and Henley all stand taking in the scene and make eye contact with each other. A look of longing, sadness, and happiness all pierce through their veins as neither of them make a move. Henley can feel the same pleasure she always got from looking at Levi. Henley can feel her heart start beating faster as she still sees the handsome charm in his face. Henley sees Berkley gaze at her as Henley feels a sense of relief as she knows she will always have her as family. The trio in that moment says so much in just their eyes.

Henley's eyes go past Levi to see a familiar sighting, a sighting that unnerves her. Berkley seeing Henleys eyes widen follows her gaze as she sees shadows surrounding the trees behind Levi. As Levi is taking in this moment, suddenly seeing the overwhelming look in the girls' eyes and Henley uncomfortably adjusting her eyes to try to make out what she is seeing behind him, to Berkley making a silent gasping sound as her eyes change from love to an incredulous look.

Levi turns to face whatever is leaving them in shock. He turns around, placing his back directly to Henley and Berkley as the trio stare at an image that is familiar that is overcrowding the oak trees. As they all stand in complete horror and utter disbelief, they see the four people among the crowd that changed their lives. The four people who took everything from them. The four people who are completely responsible for the way the trio views the world now.

Old Man Jones, Sad Eyed Sally, Rambling Ronnie, and Freakshow Freddie all beaming with joy as they secretly watch the group of people disperse. The town that believes nothing could happen, or nothing could go wrong finally learned that nothing was ever as it appears. Sad Eyed Sally leaning against her cane propping against the tree has finally let go of the pain and hatred she had for the town. Henley can see that Sad Eyed Sally doesn't appear so full of hate anymore. Rambling Ronnie sitting on the black bench underneath the Oak Trees grinning cheek to cheek. Henley making eye contact with Rambling Ronnie realizes that he just simply wants to be remembered. And on Halloween night he made sure to accomplish that goal. Because ultimately, they could never forget him. Freakshow Freddie sitting on the bench next to Ronnie has a look of pure joy in his eyes. Henley thinking back to Freakshow Freddie and how he just wanted a family. Henley feels a sudden coldness run through her veins as she realizes these four killers in a very disturbing way are family to one another.

Old Man Jones, the mastermind behind this whole creation looking upon his favorite trio leaning his shoulder against the tree with his briefcase sitting at his feet. Henley wondering if any of their actions that night had made them sad. Was there any sleep lost between the four killers? Or did they just not care? In that moment, as she looks at Old Man Jones, she feels that he is sad. However, Rocky River, Wyoming had created such an environment for these four individuals that in their own disgusting weird manner, they set out to show the town that even with all their rules in place even the best intentions can lead to a horrific scene.

Old Man Jones needed this town to have a foundation of commitment to help people out of their own nightmares. Sad Eyed Sally needed this town to truly believe and support one another even in horrendous times. Rambling Ronnie had to instill the fact of trust in this town so no one ever had to feel the pain of no one believing you. Given that the kids that survived are able to go on with their lives without being questioned or ridiculed all the time, shows this town is willing to support the unknown now. Lastly, Freakshow Freddie brought family to the table because no one in this town should ever have to feel alone.

The town has come to the recognition of their lack of care towards the townspeople. Henley looking at the four killers knows they believe their job is complete. A devised plan to create a town of commitment, love, trust, and family. A town that the infamous four all needed individually throughout their lives.

Henley seeing Old Man Jones glancing at the family he created as the four are just beaming at the trio. Old Man Jones tips his hat down, picks his briefcase up, smiles his devilishly grin and silently leads the infamous four to disappear amongst the crowd.

Henley watching Old Man Jones disappear, she feels a sense of relief. As much as the four took from her that night, she knows deep down somehow, they were affected too. Their actions as brutal and unreasonable as they were, help instill in Henley that life is precious. No matter your age. Henley watching a man that gave her so much horror as he turns his back to her, she knows in that moment the town will be safe. The town will not have to endure what she and her friends had too, in some sick twisted way Old Man Jones completed what he set out to do. And if Henley has to endure the pain and suffering to prevent future teens from suffering the same fate that is something Henley will take on. As long as her hometown is safe, and the four never come back Henley can leave in peace.

The End

About the Author

Elexa Wood born in a small-town in Texas and she currently resides in Utah. She graduated from Texas A&M University. When she isn't deep diving into the scary movies, she finds a little time to write. This is her debut novel.

Printed in Dunstable, United Kingdom

72523280R00092